My Stalker

Kendl Porter

Contents

ONE

I didn't stop running as someone was following me their scent was everywhere which was driving me crazy, it was late at night and I knew this would happen

I was sure it was my stalker, after 2 years he still hasn't gone got no one else but me the gate to my house was locked leaving me no option but to climb

Jumping over and running to my house as I looked one last time there he stood standing in all black staring at me

It gave me the chills so I quickly entered my house everyone of course sleeping I ran up to my room locking my door

I wasn't so scared since this happened occasionally every week, I contacted the police and even they couldn't do anything they gave me options but those still didn't work

I wanted to know so bad what this person wanted from me but I don't have the nerve to ask them, I wasn't safe anywhere and it was annoying to the point where I almost took my life away

They were obsessed with me ...

I laid on my bed cuddled into my blankets and pillows when I get a notification it was from an unknown number

?- you sure run fast...just never fast enough to get away from me I'm sure your wondering what I want from you

After all this time this fucker has the audacity to say that could of been at day one but no finally now, he already had my number so why wouldn't I text back right

Y/n- yes what do you want and wow after all this time you bring that topic up who even are you? ?- don't worry about who I am sweetheart and isn't it obvious.. I want you Y/n- we'll then don't get your hopes high because you can't have me your a dang stranger and creep ?- one day Y/n- one day what!Y/n- HUH!?!? Y/n- answer !!!!!!Y/n- hellloo who are you

They never responded after that which got me frustrated but what did they mean by one day it just stayed in my mind leaving me with a few hours of sleep

I sighed and drifted off to sleep.....

Morning

As I woke up to my mother shaking me I yawned and fully opened my eyes in confusion " you got a boyfriend and didn't tell me ?" I gave her a confused look as to what she meant by boyfriend

Y/n- huh I'm single Mom- then what are these flowers and here on the note it says it's for you

My eyes widened as I snatched the note from her hand and read it

Note: hope you love these ..to kim y/n

My mom waiting for an explanation as I didn't know what to say she doesn't believe about my stalker even though I've shown her enough proof

She thinks I'm using it as an excuse now

Y/n- even if I try to explain you won't believe me so you know what mine your business Mom- I want a grandchild so hurry up and give me one Y/n-MOM

Later Me and my friends decided to go out and get food together and I agreed because why not, I immediately got off my bed and went into my closet to look for clothes

(you can choose to wear this one or your own:)

After getting changed I did light makeup and left my house as we lived pretty close to each other we just met up and walked the rest of the way which wasn't too far

We stopped by a convenience store and got snacks since we wanted to go to the park to walk and talk, my friends don't know about my stalker and I don't want them too knowing them

Their so judgmental they would stop being friends with me and think it weird, I don't know why I'm even friends with them but whatever

They " forgot" their money at home so I was the only one left to pay as I scanned each item looking at the total I almost left them there, they think I'm super rich because my dad works at a wealthy company

As I swiped my card it said declined I was confused and tried again but it once again said declined I could hear them whispering which got me annoyed

I looked at the worker very embarrassed when suddenly a hand popped out of no where and swiped their card as it went through

That made me even more embarrassed I immediately bowed thanking them looking up I couldn't see their face but just watched them walk away

Their scent seemed so familiar but from where? I just shrugged it off and got the bag full of things and left with the girls following me from behind

We went to the park and of course it the first thing they have to mention

Liz- y/n why did your card decline?Y/n- idk it happens you know Claire- that's embarrassing though Y/n- don't you feel embarrassed making your friend pay every-time because you left your money Liz- your lucky that guy paid for you Y/n- just for me? Most of this is yours Claire- besides the point he smelled good was it just me

They talked a lot which made me doze off as in the distance I could see a talk figure in all black staring my way that's when I knew it was my stalker

He removed his hoodie as he held it up for me to see as he let it drop to the ground and he ran away, I got up running towards over there to see the hoodie on the ground

I picked it up and the aroma was for sure him as I looked everywhere he wasn't here or it was what I thought he was hiding as he watched me

I made my way back to them as they didn't even realize I was gone, such good friends right

I examined the hoodie as it was plain grey I don't know why he did this, I felt like I was watched in every direction which bothered me so bad

Y/n- I'm heading home you guys can come to my house later if you want

I didn't wait for their response as I sped walked home not stopping, as I walked in my father was having one of his meetings in the living room which didn't get my attention

As I reached my room I threw the hoodie on my couch as I jumped on my bed to just go on my phone, I heard a very soft knock on my door

I got up to see who it was but no one was there it probably was just a thud and I confused it for a knock

I just left it there and went back to my phone

Two

Night You and your family had just finished eating dinner when your friends decided to come you didn't mind but your brother crushed over them

You guys went to your room and just chilled there for a few minutes until it was just boring

Liz- I'm bored anyone else?Claire- same y/n your boring Y/n- you guys want everything perfect like go find someone else then Liz- damn chill how about we go and walk the park Claire- Omg yes since it's night tooY/n- idk Liz- y/n cmon don't be lame Claire- yea y/n Y.n- fine

I got up walking out my room as I forgot here in Seoul it gets cold at night " Liz pass me a hoodie" she threw me one as I held it in my arms as we got out

As I looked at it my soul left my body it was my stalkers hoodie they literally waisted no time heading to the park which gave me no option but to use it

The whole time it just smelled the strong cologne which I didn't care since it smelled good, I got messages so I looked to see from who

?- you look sexy in my hoodie

I was left speechless I stopped walking to see where he could be watching me from, I didn't reply but I stayed cautious

That's when it started raining lightly I groaned in annoyance since I knew they would want to leave but rain is just a beautiful thing

The smell afterwards " Omg rain we have to leave now" they didn't even want to walk home instead called a taxi but left me there

That was the last time I was seeing them I then heard footsteps behind me as I turned around there he stood with wet hair but his face was blocked by a shadow

It's like I wanted to stay and see who he was but it still scared me since he was my stalker for two years I slowly backed up

But stopped as I wanted him to leave me alone

Y/n- I don't know how to make it more clear but leave me alone you can't have me and never will!

I just heard a chuckle but nothing else, I didn't want to be there any longer so I left home knowing he could be following me

Going inside and to my room there was a big box on my bed I went up to it as I opened it to see an expensive purse in it

Who was he and how did he have money to buy a purse like this one, i out it back in the box and placed it in the corner

I got my phone and went to his contact

Y/n- can you just tell me who you are and where did you get money to buy the purse ?- you think I'm broke.. I have to have money to spoil my princess right Y/n- you can take your things back ?- was that not enough? Y/n- I told you to leave me alone and your doing the opposite ?- maybe I should make it clear to you look I'll make you mine even you don't want too so don't get your hopes to high that I'll leave you alone

I yelled in frustration throwing my phone away from me and murmuring things under my breath

I took the hoodie off going out to my balcony " I know you see and can hear me ..here's your dang hoodie back " I threw it as I landed on my driveway

Shutting the door ad I eyed the box as my brother walked in " who are you yelling at?" I laughed it off as I looked stupid

Y/n- myself Brother- oh- okay then Y/n- get out Brother- when will you get a boyfriend you seem to single Y/n- that shouldn't concern you Brother- damn who hurt you

I pushed him out locking my door

I got my pjs and set them on my bed as I removed my clothes to change into my pjs when he came to my head as I remembered

I immediately got a blanket covering myself up as I chuckled at myself for being such an idiot that's when my phone lit up as I knew it was probably a message from him

I made my way over to my phone as in fact it was him

?- seeing you like that made me act up Y/n- your a creep and weirdo ?- your cute and funny

I changed and hid under my blankets as he was typing I laid there waiting to see what the text was

?- should I come over you got me hard so you'll help me Y/n- find someone else and second of all I don't know you might ad we'll reveal yourself before I block you ?- go ahead Y/n- ok then

I blocked it which made me feel much better then what I least expected form another unknown caller

?- did you think you could go that easily your mine and forever will be Y/n- HUH nope you have something going through your head like do you need help or something ?- I told you I did need help because of you *blocks again*

I didn't know what to do at this point I've come upon him multiple times but it was now a normal thing I just couldn't live that way anymore

That's it imma get my own place in the sneakiest way ever tomorrow I'll go find apartment away from this area

?- I'll still find you

I once again was talking to myself out loud what if he just had cameras here I left my room to my bathroom

?- are you trying to hide from me Y/n- all these two years I have been ?- I can still see where you are

IN THE BATHROOM TOO HES.....been able to see me naked-

Y/n- you pervert have cameras in my bathroom ?- it's not what you think Y/n-YOU FUCKING WERIDO

Three

I woke up very early which is something I don't usually do I ran out my room I bet he was probably still sleeping just a guy living alone who steals

Just thinking of him disgusts me I got my bag and walked my way to the convenience store to get breakfast my eyes were swollen so I covered them with sunglasses

15.36

I swiped my card and thankfully it went through I took the bag and sat on the table that's already inside the store as I stared out the window to see the passing cars

I slowly ate the breakfast sandwich and my banana milk after I was done I walked the streets passing by the big buildings where the d signers stores were

And the company of Lee won the youngest ceo here in Seoul he for sure had money, I made it to the train station and got on

I sat down and waited to arrive, about half an hour later I arrived to the apartments I definitely wasn't rich but neither poor so I could maintain myself

As I walked in there was no one

Message*?- you really try to hard Y/n- your doing this aren't you ?- one day you'll understand Y/n- stop with the one day shit just get this over with you know what if you really want me so bad come get me huh or what you'll be a wussy and not do it ?- bold with your words if you insist I guess the day came

After that I never got a message from him, I was home laying in my couch as day turned into night I needed fun in my life since it was just boring at this point

A club?

It got me hyped up I'm not those girls who wear basically nothing but I'd like show my body figure and what momma gave me, every girl is different

This way I can attract more guys my brother being overprotective like always wasn't letting me leave unless he knew someone else was going with me

Brother- put on a coat it's cold outside Y/n- yes whatever now let me leave Brother- come back at 9 Y/n- it 9....Brother- one hour that's it those men can take advantage

I moved him out my way and left the house walking like the queen I am giving absolutely no fucks about anyone

My stalker eh fuck him too he can continue all he want I'll live my life while he wastes his time on me, as I arrived to the club there were a decent amount of people here

I showed my ID and I was let in surprisingly already as I entered I had eyes on me, I sat near the bar and ordered a drink

Y/n- water please

At my age I wouldn't drink even though I could I just don't like the idea of it, I felt someone sit next to me

?- let me take you out in the dance floor I can't such a gorgeous girl like you sit here alone Y/n- you want sex aren't I right ?- why assume so quickly Y/n- club men always do so go to another girl I'm not like them

He then came in front of me holding me by my throat and pulling me closer to his face " look you slut no one ever says no to me so fix that attitude of yours and let's dance "

I looked at him right into the eyes and he didn't expect it I slapped him as hard as I could and ran out of there, running in heels made me even slower I was scared he would catch up to me which was what happened

I felt someone grab me by my hair and pull me back " you thought you could get away with that ?" He raised his hand to hit me when he was hit in the back of his head with something

I fall to the ground where I see multiple feet as I feel dizzy and feel an injection as I black out

Four

Y/n pov I slowly opened my eyes as they felt heavy I head was dangling as I looked at my lap my vision being blurry but not as much

I realized I was sitting on a chair with my hands tied in the dark but the moon being the only source of light and I was for sure not at my house

The scent here was different that's when I see an elevator open right in front of me the doors open as a figure is standing there in black dressing pants and a white dressing shirt which was unbuttoned half way

I looked back down as I felt numb and weak I heart distant footsteps which got louder as they got closer to me i saw a pair of fest in front of me

The person squatted to my level I felt a hand lift my chin up as I came face to face to the most handsome men I've ever seen

Found my new crush but I didn't forget the fact that I was in such a situation, he smiled at me as I looked away totally not blushing

He then got closer to my ear which was making me freak out " you're mine now" my blushing over this guy suddenly took a stop as this scene was similar to my stalkers

Y/n- who- ..are you ?- Lee Jake or should I say your stalker

My heart stopped beating as I finally came across the men who as been stalking me for two years and had me in his home tied up but looks extremely hot

There's more to this men that I didn't know but one thing was I needed to get out of here for sure, I didn't look back up to him my feet were getting cold

To see myself barefoot

Jake- are you just going to say nothing

As he seemed distracted trying to get my attention I talked non sense to him, I untied my hands and waited for the perfect time

Y/n- where's the door? Jake- over there

I looked up to see him pointing at the elevator I was definitely not escaping knowing it will take forever, to open and then close but it's worth a shot

I got up and pushed him the elevator was like a few steps but sadly I stepped wrong and rolled my ankle I fell down as I was in pain

It wasn't a bad roll but it hurt since it would probably swell up, he chuckled as he walked closer to me " nice try " I rolled my eyes

He picked me up bridal style, he picked me up with no struggle " put me down " and he did as I said he put me down back on floor

Y/n- you see what you make me do Jake- you're the one who tried to run away Y/n- who wouldn't? Jake- idk every girl would love to stay with me Y/n- we'll I'm not those girls

I sighed and once again picked me up as he walked into the elevator, none of us said anything I just admired his side profile

Sharp jawline, neck full of tattoos and such a beautiful nose I was probably staring at him for too long that he glanced over while smirking

His light brown eyes could kill any girl and including me, the door opened as we reached what seemed like the first floor

There was nobody but every light on and designed well we reached the outside as it was cold I don't know why I stayed in his arms if my intention was to get away from this guy

When I saw the car we were going to I was shocked and speechless I really needed to know what this guy did for a living he seemed rich

He opened the door and put me inside in the passenger seat I stopped him from closing the door " your taking me back home right " he nodded and shut the door

Something seemed off about him his aura was different but it's like I didn't mind it, he drove and it looked familiar the streets and shops only when he took a different turn

Y/n- this is not the way to my house Jake- oh wait sorry not your house but mine Y/n- your fucking with me I'll jump out this car right now Jake- go ahead do it hopefully you'll make it home Y/n- fine

I slowly grabbed the door handle but I didn't do anything I was obviously not going to jump out especially at the speed this fucker is going at

I would not make it home...

Jake- yea I thought so

I was now fucked I was just thinking of all the things he would do to me and that he probably has like twenty girls kidnapped in his basement and I'll be one of them

Y/n- why do you want me so bad? Jake- I'll explain later

After some time in the car we were in the rich neighborhood with massive mansions, did he really live here he probably lived with his parents and does stupid things

The gates opened when my brother popped into my head it was past midnight he's probably looking for me and things while me here in an expensive car and that I was kidnapped appeared in some hot guys house

I felt the car stop as he got out the car and walked to my side of the car my ankle being swollen up already he picked me up out the car as he walked towards the house

As the doors were open by guards they immediately bowed as other guards and maids did the same

Jake- bring a bag of ice to my room Maid- yes sir

Five

We entered a room which I assumed was his I liked the vibe to it, he set me down on the bed I avoided looking at him as I stayed silent

From the corner of my eye I saw how he sat down on a chair next to the bed that's when the maid came in with the ice bag

She then excused herself he stood up and sat in front of him he grabbed my leg but I pulled it away from him he then took it and pulled it his way

As he put the bag of ice on my ankle " look y/n you can make it harder for the both of us or just corporate with me"

Y/n- this seems like fate to you doesn't it Jake- because it is Y/n-no you kidnapped me Jake- you wouldn't just come with me

I sarcastically laughed at him " let me make it easier I go home and you find another bitch"

I got off the bed and headed to the door as I tried to open it I felt a hand on the back of myNeck as I was pulled back and slammed against the door

I felt him get very close to me " I thought I made it fucking clear you were mine "

Y/n- you don't own me Jake- you're in my hands so I can do whatever I want with you Y/n- keep dreaming you think it'll be that easy Jake- you really want to test me Y/n- sure

He still held me by my neck as he pushed me on the bed as I turned back to see him removing his shirt and getting on the bed

I backed up as I hit the headboard is stared right into my eyes as I got nervous " o-okay stop" he chuckled at me as he got up to leave but stopped

Jake- there's everything you need in the closet get changed you won't quiet yet go to sleep you need to know everything

He then left shutting the door, I looked to see two other doors I made my way to see which one was a closet I opened one door and it was the bathroom

Just by a peek I couldn't believe my eyes it was modern but just have rich vibes everything here looked elegant

I then went to the other door which I had in mind was the closet and for sure it was I once again had nothing to say because it screamed rich and fancy

There was so much in here going from clothing, shoes, purses and accessories and probably more that I didn't see

There was even more in the drawers I just saw sweats and an oversized t shirt I changed and left the room to not even know where to go

When a lady stopped me from walking anymore " come with me " I went with her as we walked through this long hallway

And we stopped in front of a door " go in " she smiled at me creepily what was with all these people being weird

As I walked in there he sat behind the desk as he stared at me intensely , " where do you want me to sit" he pointed at the chairs in front of me

I sighed and sat down , he placed papers in front ofMe as I immediately read to see what they were about, it was everything about me

Jake- I know everything about you so there's nothing you need to hide Y/n- get to the point Jake- if you say so...you'll meet my parents tomorrow as my fiancé

As I heard the word fiancé fill my ears I knew exactly where everything would go and nope this cannot be happening

Jake- my parents want me to get married as soon as possible which is why I chose you Y/n-great story but I'm too young to ruin my life for someone like you

I got up from the chair as I headed towards the door but stopped

~yes you can marry my daughter as long as you keep paying me more, she's all yours~

A tears fell from my cheek as it was my fathers voice so that's where he gets the money to buy my brother what ever he dang wants and all the family trips

Wasn't earned money...

Jake- you're own father gave me permission now you don't have a choice Y/n- I don't care what he says no one owns me Jake- should I kill luz Y/n-NO ... please Jake- come sit back down and sign this

I slowly made my way back over to him as I get now what the contract was for

Jake- to summarize this 1. You will obey me at all times 2.I'm the men you will love 3. You aren't allowed to see other men 4. No leaving the house without a guard Y/n- what's your thing with other men? Jake- nothing big but when they have to do with anything that's mine it annoys me

Right this moment determined my life I would be signing it off to some guy who seemed like a psycho and besides that a creep

He gave me the pen as I took it , I was very hesitant but now that I was in his hands I wouldn't be leaving them anytime soon

As signed my name in cursive I knew this is where everything started with him

He smirked at me which made me nervous

Jake- now go rest Y/n- something smart you say

I stubbornly walked away as I felt him staring it was guarded really well that I didn't even walk to the room back myself

Even more they locked the door, I went to the bathroom as I looked exhausted so I went to sleep not knowing what I would expect tomorrow

Six

M orning ————-

The sun shining through the window directly at my face is what woke me up, as I looked around the room hoping it would be mine but no

That's when my eyes widen at the most gorgeous thing ever..I was wearing a diamond ring everything about it looked expensive

But it was the same one I wanted someone to propose me with he really knew everything

I guess me getting married was official, as I yawned I heard someone clear their throat as it scared me it came from the corner where he sat with his legs spread out as he was shirtless

I looked away as I was getting shy knowing him it I looked at him once he would make a whole deal about it

Jake- you're very bad at hiding your expressions

He chuckled and got up walking towards me as it made my heart beat go faster , just taking a small glance

He had such beautiful tattoos all over his body I could admire him all day and never get bored, he sat on the bed next to me as he took my hand and high had the ring on that one

I squinted me eyes as I didn't want to move my finger not one bit " do you like it " he asked as I turned my head to him and nodded with a slight smile

He smiled back which made my heart melt as his dimples showed , he then got closer as he kissed my forehead and got up to leave but stopped at the door

" get changed ..something fancy you're meeting my parents soon"

I had totally forgot about that part just thinking of it scares me, I didn't know how soon but I wanted to shower so I did and blowed dried my hair as quick as possible

Well something fancy always means a dress I wanted to give off a good impression I can't imagine how they'll be, keeping in my head to take nothing personal

(you can choose this one or your own in mind)

Since outside was very sunny and just gave good and clam vibes I wanted a bright color, my other option was black but that dress could be for something else

Paring it with white heels, a maid came in as she curled my hair slightly and did my makeup very natural in assuming his parents don't like girls that wear slot of makeup but who knows

She sprayed perfume on me which smelled so good and then told me to go downstairs, I couldn't stop looking at the ring it was just stunning

As I made my way down the stairs and into the living room where he sat waiting he notified my presence and looked at me in shock

Jake- let's go

I followed behind him as we went outside to see his collection of cars, as he chose one he opened the door for me as I stepped in and he went to the driver side

He wasted no time and he drove straight to wherever we were gonna meet up, I stared outside as I didn't know where my phone went

But I needed to know

Y/n- where's my phone? Jake- why Y/n- because I need it Jake- for what Y/n- okay never mind

I just realized how short this dress was I wasn't bothered by it but was he going to make a deal about it, let's wait and find out

As we arrived to a very tall building but we didn't exact get out just yet

Jake- don't talk to no none of the employees especially the male ones and you okay along with whatever I say or do got it if not there will be consequences Y/n- geez okay

He got out the car and immediately pulled people attention which caught me off guard, he opened my door and put his hand for me to hold as I got out

Many people looked as people took pictures and yelled things which disgusted me, he suddenly intertwined fingers with me

Like he said okay along with it so I did I knew for sure he enjoyed this literally everyone greeted us I knew he said to not interact with them but I have them all a smile

As we entered the elevator there was a guy pushing buttons and things I looked at the floor because Jake kept staring at me to see if I looked at the guy

As we got out I felt hit tighten his grip as I thanked the guy ..my mistake we made it to the ceos office as Jake just opened the door as we walked in

And there stood an elder couple as they looked very wealthy, as I made eye contact with both of them I have them a bright smile

His mom wouldn't keep her eyes off me as she was impressed or something like that " wow my son was able to pull such a gorgeous girl like you "

A bit later we sat down as his parents were on the other side of the desk and me him on the other, we just talked about how we knew each other

I just added things to what he said which seemed very believable , that's when his mom is talking to me and I feel a hand in my thigh

I bite my tongue as he was teasing me going harder each time as I pinched his hand as he took his hand off right away,

His mom- so y/n what did you think when he proposed

They all looked at me as I knew I was turning red and could stutter

Y/n- we'll it came out of no where but of course since I knew how much I loved your son I said yes His mom- you're okay with getting married at such a young age Y/n- we'll even if I'm young I'll be happy to spend the rest of my life with Jake and experience our love for each other

I saw how Jake smiled the whole time I talked, finally after an hour of lying yet it felt so real for me to say we excused ourselves and left the office

Leaving that room is like being able to breath properly " you did a good job "

Y/n- I know thanks Jake- now when we get back to the lobby there will be more people don't talk to them okay just agree with what I say if I have to talk Y/n-okay

I wasn't expecting much but I was wrong not only were the workers waiting for us to exit the elevator but people with cameras

Who was Jake and why was he this famous

I felt him good my hand tighter maybe to make me feel secure, they were yelling and trying to touch Jake and I but security escorted us out to the car

Even leaving was difficult because they stood around the car and chased it down when we left " are you okay" was the first thing he said to me

I didn't reply right away as I looked at my hand which was red and had scratches on it as it played back in my head what that girl told me

Jake- how did you get that?

The one thing I didn't want him to know yet happened " oh this .. I already had it " he gave me a stern look as the more I looked at him I was making it obvious

I couldn't look at him in the eyes and be for real " y/n does it look like I'm stupid?"

Y/n- maybe

I was taking this more in a joking way since he was so serious and I couldn't take it, " you're not taking me serious are you "

Y/n- nope Jake- okay then

He then stepped on the gas driving fast he knew one of my weaknesses I hated going fast it just scares me, " sto-p.....please"

Jake- y/n youre making things hard for the both is us just be honest Y/n- I
want to go home Jake- alright

Seven

I was not expecting him to take me to my actual home after signing that contract I was stuck with him forever

We actually went to a brides and groom shop, they made me try on multiple dresses until I liked one, their were all pretty but just didn't suit my vibe

Until the last one I tried on I fell in love I chose that one and then we left, I was starving and felt dizzy from not eating

I think Jake notified too since I had took my heels off and walked the rest of the way barefoot, he then suddenly picked me up bridal style

Jake- you're gonna get hurt Y/n- how Jake- you can't step on something and plus why didn't you tell me you were tired or hungry Y/n- it's not a big deal Jake- now that you're my fiancé I'll take care of you I won't let you get hurt

It sounded like he was lying but I knew deep inside he was serious, I didn't know what was wrong with me because being with him brought butterflies to my stomach

Just being able to admire how hot he was, and when we held hands I wish the moment didn't end but at the same time I can't forget I was forced into getting married

Was he actually winning my heart or am I easy to play, I didn't even realize the tie as staring at his plumped rose lips which were so kissable

He then smirked " you love to stare baby.. need something?" I got shy and blushed

Y/n- no Jake- you sure I can't get you anything in the world you name it Y/n- I'm sure I have enough Jake- we'll I complete it Y/n- sure

As his parents company was pretty far away from his house the drive way quiet besides when he would try to talk to me

I rest my hand on my thigh I stared outside since I had nothing else to do until I feel him grab my hand I got a bit startled since it was out of no where

As I looked down to see his finger intertwined with mine all his finger tattoos and rings but mostly his veins made his hand so attractive

Y/n- what are you doing?Jake- I can't hold you're hand?

As he bit his lip and chuckled I just rolled my eyes, maybe his love language was physical touch

As we got to his house we had food since we were both starving I couldn't eat peacefully since he kept looking at me but I just ignored it

It was a Sunday so which meant he would go to work tomorrow, it was now the afternoon and he wanted to watch tv with me

So I agreed coming downstairs after I changed and seeing him in sweats and baggy shirt was a first I thought he was all about being fancy I guess not

I sat down away from him as he looked offended by it " either you come to me or I go to you" he stated as I have him a idgaf look

Jake- that's it

He got up but I had already got up running away from him as he chased after me as we both laughed but he was really fast

As he back hugged me, my back touching his chest as he was all up in my neck since I could feel his breathing against my neck sending me chills

Then he spoke with a deep sleepy voice " didn't get to far ..I can't let you go you're to precious baby " I didn't know what to say so I took his hands off and pushed him back

As he picked me up over his shoulders and ran back downstairs and threw me on the couch and he hovered me but just laid on top of me and he hugged me and played tv

He seemed innocent but was he really? That thought just came to my head

I didn't mind it but was so falling for him he's exactly my type looks and personality but the story definitely was different

Could it be that bad?

Out of no where my hand played with his hair as we both paid attention to the tv, the maids offering us drinks and food

His head laid on my stomach since I guess he was trying to be respectful knowing him he could gone higher and my dumb self would let it happen

I noticed he fell asleep since he didn't move or laugh I got the controller and turned the tv off, he was probably really tired so I tried my best to the move so he could rest

I tried to sleep but couldn't I just kept my eyes close about an hour passed and he woke up, I smiled since his hair was everywhere and he looked lost

I finally was able to get up and stretch it was around 5 pm " how long did I sleep for" I giggled softly as he was unaware of everything

Y/n- an hour Jake- I have to get going He said as he looked at his phone I was confused by what he meant by only him leaving.. to work?

Y/n- to go where? Jake- a mi-.. work I have to finish up I don't know when I'll be back Y/n- oh

He then went upstairs as I sat on the couch waiting for him to come back downstairs, he was wearing an all black suit

Jake- eat well okay Y/n- you're not gonna eat Jake- at work I will ..I left your phone on the bed so you don't get bored Y/n- ok

He then came and kissed me forehead multiple times as he deeply stared into my eyes " I'll be back okay " I nodded and he left

Eight

After I finished eating which was so lonely I was the only one who eating at the table as the maids checked up on me

I went upstairs and took my phone as I went through everything but only my mother and brother texted me

But I also received a message from min it was odd since I only knew him from high-school so not that while ago

Min- hey y/n remember me from high school? Well yea I just wanted to get in contact with you since it's been a while maybe we could hang out? Y/n- oh hello min yes I remember you and when are you available Min- I'm out the country but when I return maybe then we can? Y/n- yea sure I'm fine with that Min- great

I just stayed on my phone most of the time doing her to would normally do, until I got the idea of searching up Lee jake

My eyes widened as what I was reading he was a ceo of multiple companies owned clubs, shops and other things his parents have their own company so he was technically born into a rich family and his net worth was high

That's when many articles popped up from today I then decided to see the comments

User1- even though I crushed over jake him and her make a perfect couple User2- totally not jealous jake is winning he has such a hot girlfriend User3- she's pretty but I would look better in his arms User4- using him for money? User5 replied to user4- making assumptions you're just mad you wish that was you

I didn't know how I felt, It was later when I heard voices downstairs as I checked to see Jake in bloody clothes and a few other guys

I was terrified as I thought he was majorly hurt running up to him as I was shaking not knowing what to do

Y/n- Jake....what happened?

He didn't respond and went limping to the kitchen " he doesn't want you to see him like that so maybe you should go to youre room " a sudden voice said

It was one of the the guys that came in too, " what happened " I was so curious

?- don't worry about it just don't be near him Y/n- how could I not...

I ignored him and walked quickly into the kitchen as he had removed his shirt

Nine

F rom what I saw it looked like he had been stabbed and cut everywhere. I had a sensitive stomach but I didn't even care at the moment.

So much had happened and quickly, but knowing he was my stalker anf Actually knowing now who he is. I felt the urge to worry for him, he had showed me how much I mean to him.

As I tried to take one more step I was dragged out of the kitchen. I had felt super angry that he didn't want me to see him or be near him. So I took it legitimately, without anyone seeing I left from the back door.

It was late so that meant dark outside. I didn't even know where I was, I ordered an Uber from my phone quickly. I had to get over a big gate but I was use to that already so I ran and jumped.

My Uber had came so I got in and told him to go. Now that I could actually be able to process everything I was engaged. My stalker had me falling for him, was this even healthy and safe.

I had to talk to my mother and brother. I wanted to hug them, I wasn't clear in my own mind. I think I just felt jealous and angry that I couldn't be near him.

After a while I finally reached my town. Then my house I ran in and yelled for my parents. They were all in the living room. I locked our front door and sat down in front of them.

My brother seemed bothered by me being there. " please I just need a hug" my brother raised his head and hugged me tightly.

Me and him grew up close so we helped each other no matter what. I explained everything which took a while and my mother finally believed me.

Brother- I'm going to kill him!Y/n- No no he's not the monster you think he is Brother- he kidnapped you y/n! How do you think that's okay? Y/n- I never said it was but he's a gentleman ok. He saved me from a drunk guy that day I went to the club. Brother- He didn't even propose properly? He has to come and ask for your hand in front of me and dad!

My phone was blowing up. It was Jake.

I went into the kitchen to answer his call. His tone wasn't aggressive or anything more concerning.   " y/n I didn't want you to see me like this that's it. You took it legitimately, please come back "

Y/n- and I was worried for you that's it. We have to talk okay. Jake- yes but please come I need you.

I hung up and decided I should go back. " I have to get back but I felt the need to tell you guys, I needed an opinion too" i said to them

Mother- you're brother is right. As long as you're okay with this than I support you. But this should be done the right way y/n. Father- yes their right he should come and ask

I took everything they said positively and into mind. My brother said to text him if anything and so I would. I headed back as fast as I could. The guards checked me to be good to enter.

I ran up to the room he was in and there he was in the bed and other man around him. They all turned their heads as I stood in the doorway.

Jake- All out my princess is here! The man chuckled and left out laughing. Maybe they were close or something.   " who are they?" I asked

Jake- they work with me and we like brothers you can say Y/n- mm alright, but how'd this happen   I pointed at his stomach since it was all bandaged up.Jake- When you have a lot of power in high class, you have enemies and so things kinda went down.Y/n- We'll protect yourself better, also I mentioned earlier we had to talk. Everything that has happened for us should be done correctly. My brother said you should go ask for my hand to him and my father!

Jake chuckled when I said ^ My brother ^ maybe he didn't expect my brother to be this strict.   " you're brother said this not your father?" He said

And I nodded " my father agreed with him thought and I agree with my brother too, so if you don't then I'm afraid this is not going to work"

Jake sighed and signaled with his eyes at himself. He referred to the state he was in and that right now was not a good moment. We agreed when he was healed and felt better he could.

The next few days me instead of me helping him he had the maids take care of him. He noticed how frustrating that was to me. He saw me as sensitive I guess.

I was there by his side the whole time, his buddies from work would often come visit him and crack jokes. I was in the room on my phone but I of course listened to their conversations.

Guy 1- manny help me still replays in my head Jake- that's not funny Guy2 - it was a mission you thought you were in a video game or what?

Mission?

Ten

They kept mentioning tjings but it was all stuff I didn't know. Who was he truly besides the fact that I know he's a well known CEO of many companies.

I then later get a text from Min. Min- I'm back in town if you want to hang out soon? Y/n- oh really already and sure when's a good day? Min- this Wednesday at 2 in the afternoon? Y/n- yes that's great!

Now that I think back into my high school days I talked to min a few times but no where I would consider him a close friend. I often did catch him staring at me but I didn't think of it in the wrong way.

I wonder what he wanted too. It would be cool if I reunited with a bunch of my high school friends. The whole time jake was trying to get my attention but I was too busy texting min.

Jake- y/n! Y/n- oh I'm sorry yes? Jake- is Wednesday a good day to go to you're parents house?

Wednesday? I can make it work right

Y/n- I uh yea but in the morning. Jake- alright then good.

The rest of the time I made sure he was good. He eventually had fallen asleep so I left the bedroom, min was calling me out of no where.

Y/n- hello? Min- I'm sorry if it's so sudden but it's been a very long time don't you think? Y/n- um well yea about to be four years Min- what kind of flowers are youre favorite? Y/n- I love tulips. Min- I'll keep that in mind then, well it was great hearing you after a while. Y/n- ahha yea okay bye.

His voice got a bit deeper but other than that he sounded the same. I wondered what he looked like now, for a while I stayed in the living room.

But it was boring, my mother thankfully called me and we spoke to each other for a very long time. She invited me and jake over for dinner, I told her I would see if he wanted to go.

I went to go check on jake but before I opened the door I heard him talking to someone. From trying really hard to listen in i couldnt hear much.   " jake are you awake?" I yelled from outside the door

But no response so I walked in and he had acted asleep. For what reason I don't know, he had a computer opened next to him. From looking at it thefe were charts and at the top in bold letters.   Drugs

Why was he looking at that?. I knew he was acting asleep so I would truly test it, I didn't want to take a closer look but I was really curious.

I grabbed the computer and it had price and the amount sold over the weeks. Is this what he did on the side? Deal with drugs.

As much as I shouldn't be looking I took the computer and kinda walked off, I kept looking and it had his full name on there. He was the main maker, he had made a lot of money of this.

I could see the VIP members. It was like a market. I had felt something behind me I turned my head to see Jake standing up. I got startled and he tried taking the computer out of my hands but I backed up.

Y/n- Is this really what you do? You deal with drugs? Jake- No you're just confused just give that to meY/n- I'm not confused I saw everything and I'm aware of it all so just confirm it. Jake- Y/n it's not what you think, please just give that to me. Y/n- you've made 10 Million dollars off this, what else are you hiding? Besides being a stalker and a drug dealer? Huh!!!

He stood there shocked since I had been raising my voice at him. He was thinking probably trying to come up with a lie.   " We can talk there's no need to yell, just how you wanted to talk to me about asking for your hand in front of your parents. I ask you to talk to me and understand me."

He wasn't wrong. After all he did agree with me and is doing what I asked because it's the correct way. I sighed and turned away from him to get my thoughts right.

He respected me decisions so I should for his, but I knew how dangerous this stuff was. Him coming back injured tells me he puts himself in danger.

I was still facing away from him when I felt my back touch him. He groaned in pain because his stomach was where he had been stabbed. He moved my hair out of my neck and gave me a gentle kiss.

As he whispered,   " I need you to trust me"

I was lost in thoughts because it drove me insane how he could act this way. " I'll take that as a yes?" He said and I turned around but before I could say anything he came forward to kiss me.

I was surprised but I kissed back, it felt like he wanted this badly and he had been holding back. It wasn't for too long since he was still in pain, I helped him to sit on the bed.

I was feeling shy from the kiss so I avoidedLooking at him. I think he caught on and pulled me onto his lap. " you're gonna hurt yourself like this" I said to him but he just smiled

Jake- I don't mind, it's you after all

Eleven

Y/n- my mother invited us for dinner, I didn't give her an answer because I knew you were still injuredJake- I don't want you're parents to see me like this, I feel like they would question itY/n- They wouldn't trust me but if you don't want too then we don't have to go. Jake- I can feel you want to go so let's go. Y/n- but you'll be in pain no? Jake- it's all worth it.

I got excited and got off him since I didn't want to cause him anymore pain. We waited until it was dinner time and in the mean time, I was choosing out what to wear.

He sat on the bed and gave me a yes or no. Finally I the right one then I helped him get dressed.   " it's you're turn to drive " he said to me

I felt some type of pressure since it was one of his nice cars. I wasn't too sure at first but then agreed, helped him get in the passenger seat and get comfortable. Then got in the driver seat.

I took a deep breath. " I haven't in a while" Jake- I know you're good I've seen you drive Y/n- what? Oh yea I guess

I made sure I was relaxed and so we took off half way there I was so good at this. I think I felt too confident that I was speeding so jake reminded me.

Y/n- this is the only time I'll drive Jake- fine with me

We finally got to my parents house and I felt so happy to see them. It had been a few days but it felt weird not seeing them everyday.

I helped jake get out and all the way to the front door. " you aren't nervous?" I asked him

Jake- No the only time I got nervous was when I met you Y/n- aw really well then let's go inside

I knocked on the door the immediately my brother opened the door. His eyes widened when he saw who was right next to me. He stood there in silence until he came to hug me.

I would suppose he would greet Jake in a bold way but he just gave a smile. He took us in to the living room where my mother and father were.

They greeted jake and definitely noticed he was injured. We sat down and I also expected my brother to be the one talking but he was dead silent.

Mother- I don't want to be rude but you look hurt. What happened? Jake- i had surgery, I've just been recovering Father- Well glad to hear it went well but I did mention to y/n about the marriage thing. Jake- she told me about it and as much as I wish I could get on my knees, well I'd like it ask for you're daughters hand to be by my side.

I looked over to my brother who seemed like he couldn't focus one bit. So I whispered over to him if he was good and he nodded.

Father- It's shows how you came out of your way even injured in pain to come and ask, but I do have a question how long have you've known each other?

They knew he was my stalker but I told them to not mention that to him at all. To not make things awkward and I lied saying we knew each other but I just ignored him sometimes.

Y/n- 2 years and more Father- well in that case I agree, you can marry herMother- this is going to make me cry, but I prepared dinner for us now we can celebrate.

Thankfully he asked them earlier and not on Wednesday. My phone was ringing for a bit but I refused to answer since this was such an important moment.

When I finally got to my phone it stopped ringing. I just shrugged it off and we headed to the table, and mom brought out dinner for us.

We all ate happily, and talked. My parents were asking Jake a lot of questions and I don't know if he was getting pressured.

I knew he was business man and dealer with drugs even though he tried to deny it.

Mother- when do you plan for the wedding? Jake- whenever y/n wants, I want her to be happy with everything Father- so from your family who's there? Jake- My parents that's all Father- you're an only child? Jake- Yes, my parents only ever wanted one

They had their conversation when I created my own with my brother he still was quiet and faced down. " you're being oddly weird today? What's happened"

Brother- nothing is wrong y/n stop asking me Y/n- let's go talk in your room then? Brother- it's not a big deal Y/n- let's go cmon

We excused ourselves and went to go talk, I had to get it out of him because what was he thinking. He was pacing around the room definitely thinking hard, " ever since you saw us you became quiet!"

Brother- You do know truly what he does right? Y/n- I kinda figured it out myself why? Brother- I never told you and I'm sorry but.. he's the guy I buy drugs from.

My heart has dropped because out of all the things I never expected this. I shut the door and grabbed him by his shirt, " tell me this isn't a lie, are you fucking with me?"

Brother- I'm clean now been clean ever since you had stalker problems I thought you had one because of me. I haven't paid off my debt with him.

I let go of him and backed up because me and him being super close I really thought he would come to me for advice or help. Being addicted was horrible.

Y/n- so are you afraid he's gonna kill you? Did he threaten you? Because if he knew who I was he sure knew we were related right? Brother- I had my face hidden everytime I left the house you would see me cover my face. But he found out but I'm pretty sure he doesn't know you're my brother I was one of his least priorities

I cried because I was frustrated with him, he really sold drugs to my younger underaged brother. I was mad at both of them,

Y/n- you really want to close the door of our friendship? Because that's what you're doing right now

My phone suddenly rang

It was min

Twelve

I didn't know if I should answer and so I did, I looked at my brother in so much disappointment.

Min- hey I can't do Wednesday can you meet up right now? Y/n- uhh... I don't think I can I'm act-Min- I'll be busy the rest of the week sincerely, can you please?

I felt bad saying no and so I agreed. After I finished talking to my brother and Eating. I made sure I didn't look like I cried and we headed back down stairs.

We finished eating all but I didn't want to seem off.Mother- where did you guys go? Y/n- his room he had something to show me and so we kinda of had our own conversation Father- well eat up

I kept side eyeing him so he just stopped looking at me. My phone rang a lot and I knew it was min, before going downstairs I had to my brother to fake he had a stomachache so I could go to the pharmacy.

Mother- don't we have medicine here? Brother- Ran out Y/n- I'll go buy him some then Jake- let me go with you Y/n- no you're hurt I'll be Quick

Jake held my wrist but at the end let me go. I would go walking since it wasn't that far from my parents house. I finally answered min

Min- it's been 15 minutes y/n Y/n- I told you I would take that much time I'm free now where are you? Min- look to you're right

I turned my head immediately and there in the distance he stood, I had kind of bad eyesight so I went over to him.

He was holding a bouquet of tulips, I was shy since it had been a very long time. " so what was the rush? I'm here now" he stayed quiet for a bit just observing me.

Instead he just smiled, i noticed he had a bruise on his lip I wonder from what.   " you've gotten even prettier, how have you been?"

Y/n- umm thank you and just doing things nothing much how about you? Min- well I went out of town for my job now I'm back I heard we live near each other Y/n- oh really what a coincidence, is there anything else you need I have things to do.Min- why were you crying? You're eyes are red and puffy Y/n- I'm going to go now

Before I could turn he stopped me and put the flowers in front of me, I obviously couldn't accept them. " i- ... "

Min- let's talk for a bit longer please? I just missed your voice-

I was waiting for him to finish his sentence until I saw he was looking behind me. I slowly turned my head to see Jake pointing a gun at min.

I got scared and started panicking, Jake- I finally come across you!

Min smirked and chuckled at jake looking at him in this state meant no good for Jake.   " okay stop! Jake put that away " I yelled at him

But he wasn't listening to me, " kill me, I'm right here"

Y/n- no NO stop let's go Jake That's when I was pushed to the side as I fell to the ground, min had pushed me so Jake could shoot him.

Y/n- Jake please don't do this I'm begging you

My back was hurting since it got scraped but I didn't care about that. I got back up and got in between them. " who is he?" Min asked me

Y/n- he's my husband, why were you in a rush to see me Min- Im you're stalker too. But for Four years I had my eyes on you but you only noticed Jake. I could hear everything through YOURE phone. I knew Jake would come along too since he could do the same. WHYD YOU GO WITH HIM HUH??

Jake- Do not raise you're damn voice at her I'll put a bullet through you're head! Min- pull the trigger than! Do it or wait you can't that's why you're like this.

I think he was referring to Jake's condition. I had many questiones and needed explanations. I kept telling Jake to let's go but he didn't want too.

Min- be honest can you really protect her? Jake- I'm positive I can, you should ask yourself that because what happened to Jennie?

That got min super furious and almost lost his mind. We were causing too much noice that the neighbors came out, finally at the end we went our own ways.

Jake took the flowers from me and threw them at min, then pulled me closer to him. We then left back to my house, I didn't even know what to say.

But of course we had to act normal.

After making up more lies, we decided to go back home. He didn't even want to look at me, I should be angry at him too but I felt sorry for doing this behind his back.

Should I be angry or sorry?

I couldn't handle the silence and tension in the car so I pulled over.   " why are you ignoring me?" I said to him

Jake- we can have this conversation at the house.

I think he was aware that fighting in the car could end bad so I agreed and arrived at the house, but as I tried to help him he went by himself.

Y/n- seriously?

He nodded and kept limping. I sighed and almost left there and then. I followed right behind him in the house and all the way to his room.

Jake- we both are going to have disagreements and agreements, you can start. Y/n- why the fuck did you sell drugs to my brother? Jake- that's why y'all left to his room huh? He told you I was his drug leader? He stopped he's clean now Y/n- does it look like that's fucking matters? He's underaged Jake! Who are you really?

Jake- you know exactly who I am. Gangster you can say, and it's business y/n I didn't know he was your brother I only found out a bit ago. He's done things you aren't aware of. Y/n- I don't want to know okay! Just for the money huh?

I wanted to scream but I kept my cool and sighed loudly. " it's not just me running this, you have to understand it's a corporation in this game" he stated

Y/n- what else do I not know? You have a fucking kid hidden? Jake- I'm crazy but not that crazy sweetheart. You tell me why you would ever meet up with a dude you barely even talked too? Y/n- (sigh) I was pressured into it okay! Jake- why are you putting excuses? Y/n- you saw the messages why are you even asking? That's another thing why in the world would you do that? You knew who he was and didn't tell me?

Jake- you trust me? Y/n- yea yes I do but-Jake- there's no but's, trust and loyalty okay beautiful?

I- I need to be away from you right now. " do you really though? I told you I needed you and you need me just as much" he talked me out of things and I was stupid for falling for him so easily

Y/n- you get your thoughts together and I'll get mine

Thirteen

It had been a while since we had that conversation and so I decided to take a bath. To try and relax myself the bath had a big window that had such a beautiful view of a garden and pond.

I played relaxing music in the back and just rest my head on my arm. Almost falling asleep that's how peaceful this was, forgetting about stressful stuff.

Jake- is that from when you fell?

I heard suddenly but I didn't love my position. The bath tub was huge so plenty of space for us both but I knew he wouldn't get in.

Or so I thought

I heard how he got in and came right behind me. Moving my hair to see my full back, I didn't know what it looked like but I guess I had scraped my back.

I felt as he kissed each scrape softly, he got even closer as our bare skin touched each other. He kissed my shoulder and ran his lips across it. Until he reached my neck.

I could sort of see his reflection from the window but I kept my eyes closed to feel this the best I could. He kissed and sucked generously, at many spots until he turned me over.

He cupped my face and looked into my eyes, " you're so beautiful, I'll continue if you say so. No rush" I think I had fallen deep into his eyes and was so mesmerized.

He chuckled and was getting up to leave. He was only in his boxers and had gotten in like that. I grabbed his hand for him to stop.   " I don't mind, you're injured still that's my only worry-

He wasted no time in getting back in. He grabbed me by my neck and kissed me hungrily. Things led from there I just watched out to not hurt him.

1 hour later

It had been a while and we were in bed resting. It was late since it was night time, I tried fallen asleep but woke up again. I felt his breathing against my neck, " what's keeping you awake?" He asked

I got a bit startled since I thought he was dead asleep. " he'll come back"

Jake- he won't ever come near you I'll make sure he doesn't. Y/n- I trust you but you need to protect yourself tooJake- I can and will, stop worrying so much and rest for now Y/n- okay yes then

Next day(morning)

I was woken up by a lot of movement. It was 6 in the morning and I was so sleepy still, Jake noticed I was still awake and came to me quickly.

Jake- I'm sorry I work you up beautiful, I have to go work so go back to sleep. Y/n- I don't want you to go though Jake- I have too, I arranged something for you so you won't be bored.

He gave me a small peck on the lips and a big kiss on my forehead. I went back to bed as he turned the lights off,

8:00

I had woken up and got breakfast in the bed. The maid had brought a piece of paper for me and it was from Jake.

Note: check the side of the bed

I checked and it was a new phone. And there was a text from ^ Husband^

~ I wanted you to feel safer. Put important people in there and everything you would need. I know one of your dreams was to go shopping without a limit. I'm giving that to you since you gave him a good night yesterday :)

I blushed so hard and got excited, I put on a cute outfit. And headed out but Jake wanted guards with me, as I shopped I didn't go too crazy but just chose everything I needed not wanted.

I wanted to be petty and post on my story to see what my fake friends would say or do. And I was right they swiped and were shocked.

" HOW??? You don't deserve it"

I left them on seen and continued

After a while I did get tired, and I missed Jake and wanted to go see him. But the guards wouldn't let me I wasn't sure why so I texted him.

Jake- I'm in a meeting right now that's why you can't come Y/n- that over me? Jake- it's important business

I didn't want to keep bothering him so I didn't reply. We had a beach near us so I made the guards drive me there, they weren't too sure at first but I made them.

I told them to watch me from afar, so I didn't catch alot of attention from the people also there. It was really hot and I wanted to just jump in the water but I would get dragged out.

My phone rang and it was the guards.

Guard- Boss said to go to his office. Y/n- I don't feel like going.Guard- He said it was an order Y/n- hm. I don't get ordered around sorry

I was sitting on these stairs that led to the beach, when everyone suddenly got up because there were gun shots. I got up almost tripping and running but I didn't know where to go.

The guards were calling me over but before I could go I felt such a sharp pain on my back. I fell down on the sand, as I tried moving but it's like my whole body froze.

I see the two guards fall to the ground as well, they expierenced exactly what I did. It's like I was getting sleepy and then my eyes shut.

Jake.....

Fourteen

A little while later..

As I opened my eyes which felt almost impossible, I looked around to see emptiness. My body was badly sore but as I tried move my arms or legs I couldn't. My vision finally got more clear and so I could see I was tied down to a chair.

My body had bruises all over and scrapes, who would do this to me? Where was Jake what was going on?

??- looks like you're awake now

A talk shadow from the corner walked closer to me, I wanted to keep my eyes shut forever then see this man ever again.

Min....

Y/n- what the hell is your problem? Min- you can say problem since I'm obsessed with you. I got what I wanted now so. Y/n- I thought you shot me? Min- the pain is almost similar like a bullet, I wouldn't kill you though you're too precious darling

I head hung low since my whole energy was drained, he scooted closer to me and I wanted to back up but stuck to a chair was not an option.

"I gave you a touch of mine. So everyone knows you're now mine. Besides we look better together" he said and he had placed his hand on my thigh.

Min- I bought you even better clothes and things, all to your liking.Y/n- you're getting too ahead of yourself, you really do need help Min- which is why your here.. to help me. You see how it all adds up Y/n- Min you really don't have to do all this, it doesn't have to go this far please Min- you should've thought of that before you went with Jake! WHY HIM HUH

He started yelling in my face about why I chose Jake over him and starting just saying random things. My ears were hurting but that's all I could do listen.

Y/n- I understand you. Min- you do?

I think that got him a little excited since he got in front of me with excited eyes. " you spent a lot of your life and time focused on me to see me go with some other guy" he slowly started nodding at me

Min- it wasn't hard to understand Rifht. So why then can't you just come to me, I've known you longer I... I did so much for you

I really wanted no violence involved wish it could all be done peacefully and get an understanding of where everyone was.

Y/n- so can't you understand me? I didn't know you were there too. I've made me decision so accept it

I think that got him angry because he started panting and slapped me. I was so shocked and in pain tears really came out.

He started taking his anger out of me as he consistently hit me. I looked up at him in disbelief, if only I had gone to Jake's office none of this would have happened.

Min-no no ... NO YOUR MINE FUCK JAKE AHH

I almsot passed out with the many times I was hit, I spit out blood that's how bad it was. I managed to untie and hands and do something sneakily.

I got all the strength I could to punch him and quickly untie my legs. The door was opened and as I tried running my legs gave up. But I had to keep pushing.

So suddenly I was pulled back by my neck, " Let me go " I yelled and tried getting him off but it was a struggle.

Jake's pov

I had informed the guards to tell y/n to come. I didn't want her to get sad and make it seem like I didn't want her near me.

I sat in the meeting room trying to focus but I was just so excited to see her. That's when multiple of my man barge in and inform me they had taken y/n and shot my two guards.

The anger that built up inside me was nothing I've seen before or felt. I stormed out of there and got my gang together, I failed at keeping her safe. I was the one to blame shes probably hating me right now.

I got armed and headed over to where I knew he would be. He better not have laid a finger on her or this will become war. I sped on the gas Petrie to waste absolutely no more time.

If he really wanted her he would obviously not kill her or if he knew she was mine. Then none of us could have her did he kill her.

We arranged a plan on the way there and I knew he must've set up some type of plan. We all spread out and made our way in, but we were wrong they weren't here.

Jake- Find them now

I said to my man who could locate them Quick. This time he really did use his brain, he was being smart about this. How could I fall for it.

I'm coming to save you y/n !

Fifteen

Y/n pov

It felt like forever being here, I was stuck in mins eyesight. I think he had the house on guard, I was waiting for Jake to come I knew he would.

Y/n- your not a real man, you can't get tjings this way Min- shut up, I'm staying focused. Y/n- jake is going to come soon, just let me go at onceMin- that's funny because I managed to trick him, it will take time in the mean time I'll have my fun.

I didn't know what he meant by that. But I got scared, he made everyone in the room leave. I had so many thoughts running in my head I didn't want them to be right.

He made his way to the windows where he closed the blinds where it made the room darker. I couldn't him see him anymore, it was getting darker outside too.

I started panting out loud since I was afraid of what he was going to do. That's when I hear his voice from behind me, " I want to treat you right too, I'll make you mine I don't care what no one has to say" he said

He placed his hands on my face and pulled my head back, I knew we were looking at each other but barely Able to see.

He planted a small kiss on my nose, " you remind of a pink flower, even smell like one"

Y/n- I'll never be yours, NEVER

I was expecting to get hit but instead he stayed quiet. " I want you to see me soft side " he said in a soothing tone.

Y/n- after what you did to me? You almost killed me, no one will want you that way.

His hands traveled past my shoulder and chest, touching my stomach. " soon in here there will be a mini you " he had really lost his mind this time.

Jake??? Where are you...

He got his hands under my shirt and lifted it up " I'll pleasure you better than him" but before min could do anything more the main doors swung open.

Min got startled as well as me and it was his guards wanting him jake was here. He got me up and we tried running but I was tied. He picked me up and ran but with my knees I kicked him in the stomach.

He dropped me to the floor and I hurriedly untied myself. I saw a glass vase and picked it up and pointed it at him so he couldn't come closer.

Jake had finally rushed in and saw the situation, min wasn't armed so he didn't have anything to defend himself. I saw jake aim at min but I stopped him, that's when a bunch of mins guards rush in.

I pulled jake and we ran up the stairs while getting shot at but didn't get hit. We were upstairs and didn't know our way around. He tried to stop and examine me but there was no time for that.

We locked ourself in one of the rooms. While they banged and tried knocking the door down. " I'm sorry I took so long, I was just loosing my mind" jake said to me

We were both trying to catch out breath, I gave him a smile to reassure him everything was okay. He then hugged me tightly but I backed him up because my body hurt.

He noticed all the bruises and his face dropped and he looked furious. " let's go out through here" i said and went out through the window.

And it took us to the roof, I was behind him and since it was raining badly. My foot slipped.

Before anything jake grabbed my arm, I looked up at him in fear. He pulled me up and over to the top, and kept my in his arms for a bit as the rain fell on us.

Jake- you're never leaving my arms ever again Y/n- let's get out of here

As we got up to leave and find a way down. Jake looked at me once before going but all of a sudden he switched sides with me as a loud BANG!

Jake fell into my arms, blood was gushing out. Min had shot him, he the evilest smirk on his face. He ran off the roof and blew me a kiss.

I shook jake for him to say something to me, we were both covered in blood, I yelled as loud as I could in pain. My face was filled from raindrops and tears,

Y/n- please please, I beg you jake don't die on me ...JAKEE JAKEEE PLEASEEEE AHHHH..

I saw the gun from afar and these thoughts in my head weren't healthy. I went over there and grabbed the gun, I saw min struggling to get back into the window and pulled the trigger.

BANG!

I don't feel guilty

Sixteen

- -

As it kept raining, I had thought I killed him but I missed. He managed to get in before the bullet released.

So many of his man came to get him, taking him to the hospital. I was injured but not as bad as him so I didn't want to be treated I wanted him too.

I knew he could make it.

Y/n- he won't die right?Guard- the possibility is high, he got surgery not too long ago. He's been through this before and turned out just fine.Y/n- I wanted to keep my hopes high he would be alive.

I couldn't sit here and be useless. I needed to do something I felt like getting revenge. I wasn't like this, violence wasn't my thing but min really set something off in me.

The pain was unbearable that I had my family come. They rushed and comforted me, " he will be okay sweetie don't think about it too much" my mother said but how can I not think about it.

He blamed himself but truly this was all my fault. He's always saving me but never me to him, I prayed and prayed he made it.

Brother- It's Jake, he'll make it and I promise you thatY/n- how would you know? Brother- I brought him once here too, I don't know if he's really told you our history. Y/n- I want you both to tell me later but I need to kill min Brother- Don't get your hands messy y/n, this is no game for you. Jake wouldn't want you too. He has poeple for that and their already doing it. Y/n- what do you suppose I do? Sit here and be useless and wait to hear if my husband is dead or alive. Brother- that's exactly right but instead hear he made it.

I was really loosing my mind, I walked the hospital. In other rooms were Jake's mam who had been hurt but not as badly as jake. I felt the need to check in on them at least.

As I went back I saw the doctor talking to my family. I ran over there and waited to hear, " you're husband... Made it. A lot of blood loss but he will be fine, a lot of resting will do the trick"

I cried of happiness, hugging everyone to hear such exciting news. I was the first one to go see him, I had to wear this blue suit. Seeing him through the glass window and then Acrually going inside.

I went by his side. Of course he was still alive and breathing, I wanted to hug him and kiss him. But I couldn't, I touched his hand as it was cold.

I was always the cold one and he was the warm one. He always made sure i was warm, this time it was my turn to make him feel my warmth and love.

I kissed his hand as a tear fell on it. " you sacrificed yourself for me way to much. Stop being dumb and let things happen. You should've let me get shot, your more important than me" I cried quietly

Seeing him in this state was not the best thing. I was theb asked to leave since my turn was over. Jake's parents had also come and we were all sad but happy at the same time.

Everyone got their chance to go visit him, since this hospital knew jake and how much power he held they respected us. Jake was transferred to a medical room in his house.

Everyone stayed to talk and questioned me what had happened. I really didn't want to talk about it because it made me feel bad.

Y/n- he got in the way so he could get shot, it all happened so fast.. i Mother- maybe we shouldn't ask her this can really be triggering for her Mother in law- you're right. Y/n it's not your fault okay. My son chose to save you so don't blame yourself

I guess they all had a Point right. It was about 3 in the morning by now, I didn't sleep or more like my body refused to sleep. I had to keep an eye on Jake afraid something else could happen.

I just stared at him laying on the bed. I wanted to talk to him, hear his voice, see the way he looks at me with those eyes.

While later

Jake POV

Getting shot wasn't a problem for me but I did have a bit more fear since I was in surgery and maybe that could interfere with this. The last thing I remember was falling in y/ns arms.

My eyes were closed and my body shut out. I could still hear her screams, they were distant though. The rain falling on my face was cold.

As I laid there I then hear another bang, my heart had dropped again, did he shoot y/n too? That's when I passed out.

Waking up again I was in a hospital room. I could only lightly open my eyes, I had made it not surprising but thankful.

My body temperature was freezing but I felt someone warm hand. That instantly made me warmer, it felt like they passed love over to me.

It was a females voice

Ive heard before. The sweet voice giving me a lecture to stop sacrificing myself for her. I knew who it was, her blush pink cheeks, cutest eyes ever and smile to die for.

My precious y/n

My body was still recovering so I fell asleep out of no where. I had a dream that turned into a nightmare where y/n died in my arms. Never would that happen.

That dream felt like it lasted so long because when I woke up again and with a bit more energy. I was in the medical room in my house. Someone was holding onto my hand, as I looked to my side

It was y/n

She was sleeping so peacefully, who knows how long she stayed up. I didn't want to lvoe my arm because that would cause her to wake up.

I needed her by my side forever

Seventeen

I just admired her beauty, but I suddenly got flashbacks of what had occurred. I knew my gang had my back but I wasn't yet informed on what else had happened.

Slowly y/n woke up and she had bags under her eyes, she was extremely tired. " I went to sleep?" She questioned and I just chuckled because she was so cute just waking up.

Y/n- wait... YOUR AWAKE!!!

She jumped out the of chair super surprised. I don't think she could believe what she was seeing, I wish I could jump with her too.

Jake- I didn't do too bad right? Y/n- don't ever do that again. Stop being dumb Jake- I saved you, that's all that matters Y/n- it's my fault this happened. ... thank you so much but please don't ever put yourself at risk for meJake- your welcome and I'll listen to you for everything else but this. I told you I would protect you until the end.

Y/n POV For now it was just me taking care of him. I didn't mind doing that, I stayed by his side whenever he needed help. To eat, sleep and other things.

Jake- I'm sorry I'm making you do this Y/n- why would you be sorry? I'm returning to you for doing that for me.

A bit later

I knew I shouldn't be getting involved in things like this but I wanted too know. Jake's gang members were here at the house discussing matters.

I leaned against the doorway to listen and see what they were talking about. " Lee Min is trying to flee from here but due to many accounts of murder, theft and much more it's become complicated for him"

Guy 1- then that will be our chance to attack, do you really think he knows this has become war? Guy2- Wether he knows or not he knows deep inside he made one of the worst mistakes in his life. Guy3- We'll take revenge for Jake. Not matter what

They had planned things out, I thought maybe this was my opportunity to join in. " he tricked you the first time, what makes you think he won't do it again?" I said

It went dead silent

They all turned their heads at me like I was some imposter. I think they were too shocked and confused what I was doing there.

Guy1- you shouldn't be here. You should be by Jake's side. Y/n- Just by his side? Is that really all I'm useful for? Guy2- you really don't know what you're talking about, this isn't a game y/n. It's real life Y/n- I realized that when Jake was shot. I'm not scared no more, I want to defend Jake just like you guys. Guy3- Miss, why don't you go bake something does that not interest you? Y/n- Of course you would say that. Put my skills to the test.

They were definitely debating it. But I managed to convince them, Jake would not allow me do this at all. But I want to prove to him that I'm capable of being able to protect him as well.

They took me to a shooting room where they gave me a target to shoot at. This was my second time holding a gun, the first time was to kill min but clearly I failed.

I knew I wasn't good, but if I told them that they wouldn't even bother talking to me.

Guy1- just breath and shoot Y/n- I know!

I got a got a good grip on the gun and aimed it. It was a glass bottle, if I didn't shoot it I would be done for. " in how many bullets should I break it?" I asked

Guy2- 1 Guy1- don't listen to him, but if your truly good 1-3 just try your best

I pulled the trigger and hoped in those few seconds I traveled through the air it would break. I shut my eyes in embarrassment knowing it didn't break.

(glass shattered)

I opened my eyes back up to see how the glass bottle was broken into bits of pieces. " not bad" they all said and continued giving me all types of tests.

Some I didn't get the first time but almost right away. That's when they all go silent and place their heads low. I turned around to see Jake standing there eyeing me down.

I had the gun in my hand, I put it down but didn't know what to do. Obviously I couldn't lie about this but maybe lead something else to it.

Jake- all of you get out.. and Now!

I thought that meant for me too as I walked he put his hand out without looking my way. I sighed knowing I wasn't going to get out of this. He would understand me though, he isn't harsh on me.

Jake- what were you thinking y/n? Y/n- what do you mean? I just wanted to watch how guns worked. Jake- oh really shooting up glass bottles and using a dagger seems like you were JUST watching.

So he had been watching this whole time....?

Y/n- it's not a big dealJake- Acrually yes it is y/n. I don't want you to ever hold a gun or have the idea of gaining interest in this. Y/n- You can't stop me from doing this! Why won't you let me? Jake- I don't want you to get your hands messy for me or anyone. This isn't the world you want to get yourself in! Y/n- I'm in it already! I'm by your side, your problems are mine too!! We can do this together just have trust

Do you trust me?

Eighteen

He really didn't want me to get this involved. But I knew he could trust me in doing this good. I had the confidence to proof we can be a team together.

Jake- I'm not going to change my mind. The decision is set, I love you too much to let you do this.Y/n- why can't you trust me, and let me show you.Jake- I trust you with all my heart. But this is not about trust, this is too dangerous. You can put your family at risk.

I feel like if it kept insisting he would get frustrated and angry. I needed to find another way but how. " just how you told me you would love, take care of me and especially protect me. I can do the same Jake , what ever it takes and I'm serious " I said

Jake knew what he had decided and he was going to stick to it. It was a bit after that we were at the dinner table eating. There was much silence and awkwardness going on.

I was thinking too much I still hadn't eaten anything from my plate. " are you not going to eat?" Jake had asked Y/n- i will

It was just us two at the table too. " if your trying to come up with something to convince me it's not going to work " he stated

He knew what I was even thinking too. This was going to be harder then ever, maybe it will have to be sneakily .

The rest of the night I was on call with my brother, I figured maybe he could tell me something helpful. " Y/n I agree with Jake, you don't know what your getting yourself into. Just stay out of it"

Y/n- I thought you were going to be more useful then this, you should have given yourself that advice being messing with drugs Brother- dang that hurt and I'm clean now. I'm not like that and I regret it all the time. By the way when do you plan on getting married it's been time

All of this made me forget about my marriage with Jake. So many people kept telling me to stay out of it and I don't know if that was a sign or not. For now I would just stop and let it flow.

But if I have the chance i would for sure kill min. That was my only goal, I didn't want nothing else but that. " you're right I might as well start planning it"

No wedding before he's dead though.

I was outside in the balcony while I called my brother so I went back inside to where Jake was sitting on the bed on his computer.

He was using his glasses and he looked so fine. This was the man I was marrying? He seemed so focused on work so I got in the bed next to him and just stared at his side profile.

He faced me and got shy. " why are you staring at me with those eyes " he said

Y/n- I'm in love with you that's all Jake- can you prove it? Y/n- in many ways.

He placed his computer on the side and came closer to me and hovering over me. " you're still healing Jake "

Jake- I didn't say I was going to fuck you, you just look good waiting for me to do something Y/n- then why keep me waiting?

He chuckled but before we could do anything, someone knocked on our door. I got out off underneath him startled.

He went to the door and I could barely see but it was a man in a all black suit. Wearing sunglasses and they talked super low. It took a few minutes but it seemed serious.

Jake came back in after shutting the door and straight to his closet. He was getting clothes and out them on. " where are you going?" He looked up and thought about it but didn't say anything to me.

Y/n- are you just going to ignore me like that? I asked you something Jake- go to bed and don't wait for me Y/n- that's all? What else do you need me to do huh? Jake- stop asking questions.

After Being done changing he got guns, " Jake I'm serious tell me what's going on?" He stopped and walked over to me, grabbing my face and smiling at me.

Jake- you look tired so head to bed okay. I'll be back, I love you

He came closer to kiss me but I didn't want it to end. Then one kiss on my forehead before leaving. " wait wait " I said

Jake- I have to go okay He shut the door, I sprinted over to it. Trying to open it but it was locked. I yelled for him to open it and hitting the door made no difference.

What was happening ?

Nineteen

I kept banging on the door and yelling which brought me to tears. He had barely healed and now he's going back out to do business or whatever.

I think I sat against the door for half an hour before I gave up. I was in the shower letting the water really soak me, I thought really hard what he could be doing.

I felt suddenly angry so I got out the shower and got changed in all black. I re traced his steps but it was an empty parking spot.

I feel like he knew I would find a way to come out and follow him. Think y/n think hard, don't let him trick you. I brought his laptop with me, and it showed his phone was connected to it.

I checked his phones location, and it was a building. I drove in slowly and quietly, parking a bit away. Having to go through the woods to get there.

I walked like nothing and got against the wall. Please Jake be in here and don't die. I got in through a door and hid, and I was right there were in here doing some type of business.

Guy- if you really need my help you'd have to give me something obviously right. How about the girl. Jake- what girl? Guy- The one with you, I mean after all it's just a setup right? Jake- at first, not anymore. I fell in love with her ever since I met her. Guy- oh really what do you think she'd say if you told her the truth? Jake- I don't know and I don't want to know. But she's not an option. Guy- we'll make it a choice because that's the only thing I want.

What set up?

I couldn't believe what I was hearing. If to come out and confront both of them or run away from him. I was really trying to process this all that I stumbled backwards and dropped boxes.

I hid on the other side hoping they didn't catch me. " it was just a raccoon, I'll take it outside " I saw this dude pass by me and I had to hold in my breath.

After a bit I went by the door again, through out the mean time of them discussing their options. I felt breathing on my neck, maybe I was not focusing and just felt frustrated.

???- gotcha!

I felt a piece of cloth go over my nose, I tried yelling but no one would hear me. My eyes slowly shut as I was passing out. That's when it all went black.

Quick Jake pov

I was here doing business with Laro, since I knew he had one of the best security teams. My and his family worked together years back and met that way. I was hoping he would continue to be help but I guess that changed.

He wanted y/n

The only thing I would not let go especially to the hands of this guy. He was exposing everything that had happened, the only reason he knew was because he and his gang hacked into my system.

Afterwards we took major pro caution, I didn't want y/n to find out. This would kill me and even more of her, her heart would be shattered into millions of pieces.

But I wanted her to know I was taking her serious. This wasn't for no stupid rule, I actually wanted her to be mine. My eyes saw who she truly was, this fake personality wasn't fake.

I always wanted to treat her like a queen. I really hoped she would never find out. This would ruin me.

Out of no where we hear stuff fall from a room behind us. We both turned and made our man go check it out, turns out it was just a raccoon.

Not a bit later. I hear mumbling again from that room but I tried really not to care. His man had come up to Laro and whispered something into his hear. And he smirked while chuckling.

He picked up a cigarette and took a good one in while letting it out. "you're a bad, bad boy Jake, you got her attached. I think she might even die for you" he said

I gave him a confused look by what he meant. He passed me the cigarette but I smacked it out of his hand. " I think she might even have the mind of a Mafia, she found out where you went. I guess we make a deal " he shook my hand and smiled

Jake- What the hell are you talking about? What deal we never made SHES NOT YOURS? Laro- I guess she came to me. After all it wasn't a raccoon just a sneaky cat. What's her name? Y/n . She was in the room and listened to our conversation

No......

Jake- What? Where is she? WHERE IS SHE? Laro- stop yelling, hmm well now that she's mine I don't think you need that type of information right.

I got out of my chair and grabbed him by the collar, " don't okay fucking games with me, you saw what I'm capable of. Tell me where she is " he acted like he was drunk.

Laro- I wanted her to get out of our way. Ever since she came into your life, you've had no uncle and nephew time. I'll take care of her for you right she was just a set up Jake- Don't call yourself uncle, your nothing to me.

I took his gun and pointed it at his head. Looking him straight into the eyes wanting a damn answer.

Laro- you won't make it in time. She here He showed me a video of y/n in a pool that was being filled up with water. But she was tied down.

I pushed him back and ran out of there, I had her location at all times. My worry was not getting there in time of course knowing she had heard everything was also a worry.

I knew she would understand, I should've known better she would have followed me. At this point I'm taking revenge on the whole damn world.

Save me...

Twenty

I started panicking and gasping for air because I felt so stupid. This was once happening again, why would she follow me.

I got there as fast as I could but the lights were taking forever. I knew I was taking a very long time, the pool could be filled up by now.

When I got there rushing inside, no one was there to stop me. But going to where the actual pool was where I stopped myself from going any further in.

Y/n was lying on the floor but the one giving her cpr looked familiar.

It was Min....

He saw me walk in but didn't stop and kept helping y/n. This wasn't a moment to fight even though I had a lot of anger for him.

We both kind of stood there in disbelief, we were both too late. " if I would've known you had created a set up I would've met y/n before you"

Is what min had to say to me. I didn't say anything back because I wasn't going to stand there and deny it. But no one will understand it's not how I truly feel about the situation.

Min- does she even know the truth? Jake- she overhead yes. This is not-Min- Were you even going to tell her? I'm no one to judge but all this to prove yourself? Jake- I see her differently, I actually fell in love with her. I have protected her havent I?

Min pointed at her state " that says it all buddy" he stated very disappointingly. That's when y/n starts coughing the water, my instinct was to help her but min stopped my and nodded not too.

It took her a few minutes to remember and recognize. Where she was. That's when she looked up at me and backed up. Even more when she saw mom next to her.

Y/n- were y'all even against each other this whole time? Min- We have and still are, that's not important right now how do you feel? Y/n- both of you get away from me. I don't want to see either of you

Min had backed up and gave her space but I needed to talk to her and truly explain. " y/n.... I'm sorry I-" Couldn't even finish my sentence without tearing up myself. I felt like trash and such a jerk.

Y/n- Jake you played your part well enough. I knew my parents were right. Jake- You don't understand- Y/n- I understand all of it jake, EVERY SINGLE PART.

She got up from the ground and walked out the building slamming the door. I was going after her but min had already done so.

Should I give her space or not let her go. I removed my wet coat and ran after only to see min wrapping his jacket around her. Then both of them walking to a car which I supposed was his.

I punched the door is frustration, I myself was turning crazy. I couldn't watch her leave with some other guy.

I ran after but they had drove away. I kept walking when I stepped on something, it was the ring I had given y/n. This just broke me even more.

I called my parents and arranged a quick meeting with them. " this isn't a set up at all, I am in love with her. Insanely in love with her, she's everything I want" I impatiently said to my parents.

Mother- you really want her go and get her.Father- I think she made us learn a lesson, be a man and don't cry. If she was really yours Whyd you let her go with him?

Twenty one

Y /n POV

The only reason I went with min was because I wanted to hurt Jake. I knew this would make him think a lot, or maybe there were no such feelings as he said.

Everything he had said or did with me was all lie. What exactly was he getting out of this, my whole life was a life at this point. I was shivering from being in the water for a while.

Y/n- Did you know it was a set up all along? Min- I'm just as clueless as you. I really thought he was as interested as I was. I'm sorry about that.Y/n- take me home.

He said nothing else and actually did what I told him to do. It's not that I've forgiven what he has done to me, but it was my only way to get away from Jake.

Everything he's given me was thrown out the window. I wanted absolutely nothing to do with him, once they do something once it's likely they'll do it twice.

When I got home I was outside for a bit since it was super late. Eventually my mother opened the door and when she saw me in my state. She gasped and yelled for my father.

From tiredness I fell into her arms and mom stopped cried. But hugged her from being cold, the door was opened and I saw min drive away.

My brother came downstairs as well as my father and covered me to make me warm. I felt like it was all a dream and that I could wake up and it all be lie.

But the truth was I was living in the lie. After a bit I got warmer and gained my strength back, " y/n you haven't said anything for an hour, sweetie what happened to you? Where's Jake?"

Just hearing his name made me angry. " it was a set up, he never truly wanted me. It was to prove himself but I still don't know everything " I said tearing up more

They all were in shock and disbelief not knowing what to say back. " who dropped you off right now?"

Y/n- Min Father- wasn't he the one who shot Jake? Y/n- he saved my life tonight, I had downed in a pool but he gave me cpr right before Jake arrived.

I went to my room which I missed. I felt like I was finally in peace, I didn't have to worry about anything. It took me a bit to sleep but eventually I did.

Morning:

It was around 9 in the morning when my mom came into my room with a tray of food. " eat you look so weak" I gave her a small smile

I missed her cooking. It brought me back to when I felt happy, my emotions over took me right now. Having no phone had benefits, I could disconnect myself from the world.

Mom- what are you going to do now? Y/n- I'm still lost, I need help I- Mom- it's okay don't think about it right now, just eat your food.

After eating my food I thought taking a walk with the fresh breeze could calm me down a bit more. It was around spring time, the trees would be blooming any minute now.

I looked dead the way I was walking so I tried walking more normal. I saw a bunch of little kids playing on the playground so I sat on a bench and observed from afar.

I really imagined myself walking down the aisle one day and getting married to the men I thought was my soulmate. My bestfriend and lover for the rest of my life.

Suddenly a kid came running up to me. Handing me a tulip, just a single one. The boy that ran away, the tulip had a piece of paper attached to it.

Note: I hope this makes you feel better

But it didn't say who it was from. I looked around but no one I knew. I learned my lesson once I placed the tulip on the bench and left it there as I walked away.

I felt like I was being watched, so I thought going back home was a good idea. " y/n"

Someone calling my name should I stop or not? I didn't know what To do I hated this. Was I just too broken, someone grabbed me by my hand and stopped me.

I was afraid to look back but I had too. The man removed the hoodie off from their head,

Ja....ke

Jake- just let me explain please, this was not supposed to go this way Y/n- THEN WHAT WAY? You lied Jake, you fucking lied this whole time. I-... IM DONE!!!

I was yelling at this point. I was taking all of my anger out on him. He finally saw how hurt this had made me, I pulled my arm away from him and walked away.

But yet he didn't give up. He followed behind me until I saw my brother run from across the street and over to me. He got in front of me and told Jake to leave.

Jake- You still owe me why are you getting involved ?

My brother got money from his pocket and threw it at him. " go get fucking drugged like that one day, you wanna show people what your really capable of?" That shut Jake up right away

Jake- y/n I really do love you, I'll always love you. Just let me explain to you correctly Y/n- fuck off! Jake- I'll do anything please

He has fallen to his knees and begged for his life. For a moment I was giving in but this was just too much to forget in a day.

Y/n- you did it Jake. You want a hug? Kiss what? You accomplished proving you're a real man, let's throw a party for you. Jake- I want you y/n. I don't care about proving to anyone who I am. Bevause I want you to find yourself through me. Y/n- wow thank you because I already did. I stupid fucking girl who fell for an idiot like you.

I truly did love you

Twenty two

- -

I started feeling sick out of no where. So I quickly got home, i didn't want to look back or more like I couldn't either way.

What was I going to do now. Definitely not go with no men, I've learned to not trust at all. Through out the day I started feeling more sick. Maybe from all the stress and much anxiety got me like this.

I told my mom everything, my brother wanted to know as well and so that brought my father in my room too. All that had happened between me and him obviously not too deep but yea.

Y/n- I should've known having a stalker was a red flag, I don't know what I was thinking. Father- Your human, your bound to make mistakes. As long as you learn from this one.

For dinner my mother made me chicken soup. I feel like that always helps people feel better and it really did. I'm a boss woman, why am I letting him get me like this.

I'm going to hurt him the way he did to me. There's no excuse after all.

Next few days:

I had gotten even worse. I was feeling super sick, weak and everything. My brother decided to take me to the doctors to see what's up. I was so nervous I don't even know why.

Brother- maybe just a stomach bug? Y/n- hopefully

The doctor came back in and had a huge smile on her face. She said it for herself and even handed me papers. My eyes widened, I gave my brother the papers and even he was shocked.

We got out of there and he hugged me so tight. " this explains you in the bathroom at 2 am " he said to me and I just laughed it off.

He became my personal bodyguard, making sure to get me in the car safely. Before we got home I told him to just let this be on the low for a bit.

When we got home my mother was patiently waiting to hear the news. " I had a stomach virus, she gave me medicine and i should be fine"

My mom nodded. I went to go buy my self a new phone, and just start fresh. I guess I would be having a blessing very soon. My life just got better.

Jake POV

I was sitting in my office super sad and annoyed. I was annoyed at everyone even if they did nothing to me. I wanted to talk to no one absolutely no one but y/n.

I could just go to her house but I don't want to be rude. I lost her forever and it was all my fault, I should've told her the truth to begin with.

That's when randomly min walks in. My guards aimed their guns straight at him but I told them to lower them.

He had the biggest smirk on his face as he came to sit down in front of me. " well before I begin on too why I even came in the first place, my throats a little dry " he poured himself a cup of whiskey and sat back down

Min- what did you think was gonna happen when she found out? You really thought she would forgive you just like those times you hit the clubs? Jake- It's apart of business, I didn't go do anything else. You've been all up in my business and for what?Min- I just wanted to see your downfall of course. I did manage to find something out myself, you really are one nasty mf.

At this point I was feeling disrespected, but what did he know that I didn't. For him to be calling me such name must mean something occurred.

Jake- Look I don't have time for bullshit, get to the damn point. Min- I know how much your thinking of her. This is gonna make you think even more. From night to day such news appeared. Jake- What are you saying?! Just tell me already. Min- we'll id like something in return.Jake- like what? Be fucking reasonable

He looked around my office but nothing seemed to catch his attention. Until he tapped my desk, " where your sitting " I sighed

Jake- I can find out myself. In your dreams buddy.Min- She's pregnant.

Did I hear him right?

I got out of my seat anf went over to him, " are you playing with me?" He chuckled

Min- I don't waste my time either. But it would fascinate me to see the look on your face after hearing. You've lost not just her but your kid too.

This can't be happening.....

Twenty three

J ake- How do you know? Did she tell you? Your not even the father and she's telling you? Min- She didn't tell me anything, I got curious and saw she went to the doctors. Then that's where I found out.

There was no form of me having contact with y/n. So I would have to go myself to her, after all that was my kid too. I got my coat and left quickly.

When I got to her house I was backing out. I waited in my car for a while, maybe she would come out. And luckily she did.

Y/n POV I had decided that I was going to continue my life without a guy. They were just a waste of time, I left my house to go look at apartments.

I loved being with my parents but soon enough, when my baby would be born I didn't want them to get woken up. As I walked down the street someone randomly approached me.

I got scared and backed up, " Why did you tell me you were pregnant?" Jake said getting in my face, I didn't know to tell him the truth or lie.

Y/n- I'm not pregnant. You really think I'd have a baby with you? Jake- Now that I remember we fucked and never protected ourselves. Y/n- Okay but I'm not pregnant I don't know where you're getting that from. Jake-Tell me the truth y/n.

I rolled my eyes and kept walking but he dragged me back. Pulling in my wrist and yelling in my face to tell him the truth. I've never seen this side of him, Was this who he truly was?

Y/n- you're hurting me Jake, and I don't want nothing to do with you anymore. Jake- that baby is my kid too, you have no right taking me out of their life.Y/n- And YOU HAD NO RIGHT LYING TO ME. You think it's fair of what you did? I'm trying to forget Jake but you keep coming back like I'm going to forgive you.

I pulled my hands away from him. " you never let me explain y/n, you think that was fair? You don't even know the whole truth and your hating on me." I scoffed

He really did sound stupid, I nodded my head in disappointment. He was just getting in my way, who told him I was pregnant?

Jake- I love you y/n , IM FUCKING IN LOVE WITH YOU! I'd kill for you, but please just listen to me. Y/n- tell me we weren't just friends than huh? Jake- I never considered you that ever, but I can't loose you and I can't see you get with someone else.

At this time I really thought if I should give him a chance to Acrually explain himself. He has been showing up for a reason, maybe this wasn't his intention.

Y/n- okay here's my number. Right now I'm busy but I'll text you when I can. Jake- thank you so much y/n.

We then parted ways. Hopefully this wasn't going to be a mistake I was making. I'm glad I was able to stick up for myself and not let him do whatever he wants.

I spent the day looking at apartments but none of them were my taste. I wanted easy access especially when my belly would get bigger. Somewhere near my mothers house too.

Next day:

I was looking at Jake's number and ready to text but suddenly I received a message from him.

Jake- Can you meet up right now? Y/n- yes I can. Jake- I'll go pick you up at your house than? Y/n- yes that's fine.

I had taken pictures pre pregnancy and just take picture through out it. That's when he had come, I don't know why I was nervous. It felt like we were in the talking stage and we were going out.

I had to be tough. I got out and went to his car. I had let me brother know just in case of anything. I got inside the car and Jake drove off.

Jake- do you mind going to my office? Y/n- no it's fine

We got to his office and a lot of people were watching us go by. They still gave me those nice smiles, when we reached the elevator..

He pressured me into going into the corner of the elevator. I just looked up at him confused of what he was doing. " I'm telling you now, I can't let you leave my side" he said looking at me straight into my eyes.

The elevator doors opened and the poeple on this floor just looked at us, like what was going on. I pushed him back

Instead of us going out the elevator he pressed the door to shut again but I opened it back up. He sighed and took my wrist pulling me all the way to his office slamming the doors shut.

He sat me down on the couch. " I really can't resist anymore y/n"

Y/n- I came here to talk nothing else. Sit down and explain to me or else I'm leaving and blocking you out of my life forever. Jake- okay ok. You know about the setup but the truth is it was for my parents. I will never be good enough for them. Y/n- your parents are nice and sweet. What are you talking about? Jake- that's what you think. They barely switched up one me not too long ago. They're ready to see me fail once again, but I don't care anymore. I just want to be by your side forever.

Forever....?

Twenty four

He was just spilling his heart out to me, to the point his eyes were getting watery. He realized I was just staring at him like he was crazy or something.

He took some deep breaths and came back to tell me more. I do take accountability that I should've gave him the chance to say something. But then when you hear something like that you don't know how to react.

I was upset he wasn't even going to tell me. He had his reasons and it was all understandable, but I still had this frustration in me I don't know why.

Y/n- we'll you didn't have to lie to me, if I hadn't listened I bet you that you wouldn't even have told me. Jake- And I told you a million times why! I only wanted the best for you, it was breaking me inside and I rather that then watch you be hurt. Y/n- Since day one! Jake day one that's all you had to do, but of course your parents were in on this. Jake- Why do you keep going back to that? I don't know how many more times I have to keep repeating the same thing for you to understand. Y/n- We'll you didn't have to lie-

He sighed so loudly and fell to his knees in front of me. And hung his head low and I could see he was breathing heavily.

Jake- IM ONLY HUMAN, WHAT ELSE DO YOU WANT? I can't keep begging you anymore, I've done everything I can and yet you still kick me out of your life. Y/n- I- Jake- PLEASE UNDERSTAND THAT IM TRYING MY HARDEST.

He was crying at this point, staring directly into me. I was lost for words, he got up and stormed out of here. I felt so bad, I got up going after him.

I grabbed his hand but he pulled it away, instead of him chasing me it was the other way around. I didn't know what to do anymore, he went into another room.

It was locked and so I had no way of getting in, the people there didn't want to unlock it. I was feeling super exhausted and weak. But my heart told me to fight for him.

I laid against the door knocking softly and whispering his name. I got tired of standing so I sat against the door, calling for him quietly.

The day was passing by, it had reached the afternoon. And soon after night, my stomach was growling from how hungry I was.

I was feeling lightheaded and so I stopped trying to wait. When I got up I fell down, no one was on the floor so I was by myself. " jake...." I said as I laid on the floor.

I pulled my phone out to call jake but he wouldn't answer, I tried yelling but I felt too out of breath. So instead I called 911, I think from not eating.

I was pregnant and I have to eat. They were on their way, finally reaching the floor number, they saw me and came to me.

With all the loud yelling anf tjings it brought much attention to jake. He came out the room and saw the way they put me on the bed. They were quick with tjings, jake called my name but I just looked at him

He got into the elevator with us and well yea. He thankfully got into the ambulance with me, I felt a warm hand touch my hand.

First responder- Her vitals are fine

We finally got into the hospital room and the nurses came to care for me. This was the same hospital jake came too. Since they knew who he was they wasted no time in working with me.

I got an IV and just had to stay there overnight.

Doctor- let's make sure to eat next time okay. Your low on vitamin D. Y/n- How's my baby? Doctor- I'm sorry what? Y/n- I'm pregnant Doctor- let's take a quick ultrasound and check then.

As she was doing the ultrasound, it was silent. It took a bit before she turned her head over to me and Jake. " did you take a pregnancy test?" The doctor asked me

Y/n- we'll I went to the doctors and they told me I was. Doctor- how long ago? Y/n- few days ago Doctor- I'm sorry sweetie but there's not heartbeat here, there's nothing visible either.

No heartbeat....

Twenty five

What??? How???? What was happening because I know I'm pregnant and I'm feeling sick so what happened.

I tried getting off the bed but the lady held me down. And called for Jake to help her, " STOP IM PREGNANT!" I kept repeating because I knew I was.

They injected something in me to fall asleep and so it kicked in and I fell asleep......

Jake pov

Was it my fault she lost the baby? I made her wait out there for too long, I made her get stressed. I should've taken care of her knowing she was pregnant. I failed her once again.

This didn't make sense how so quickly could she loose a baby. The doctor saying she was never pregnant just made everything class with each other.

Someone was lying and making up things. The only person I had to ask was min, as much as I hate seeing his face I knew he would know.

Maybe he was the liar after all

I met up with him outside the hospital and we talked. " y/n was never pregnant, why is this? " he's face went sort of blank, he stuttered with giving me an answer.

I knew I had to keep my face straight and show no emotion, he definitely knew something. " I found out the same day she did! She probably lost it fighting with you" he said like he was offended I was asking him.

Jake- do I have to beat the living shit out of you to tell me the truth? Your face as pale and you can't even hold eye contact with me. Aren't you a real man act like one. Min- Stop insulting me, if she lost the baby or whatever what does that have to do with me. Jake- because it's very weird how you found out. The doctors don't just give out personal information like that. You bribed them with money didn't you? Min- Go fuck yourself, your the problem!!

I grabbed him by the back of his hair and slammed him into the car. There weren't many people around but the workers knew who I was so of course they didn't interfere.

Jake- I'm giving you one last chance, stupid motherfucker! Min- I love to see you suffer(gasping for air) I can't let you be happy with her. I took care of her as safely as possible. Jake- WHAT DID YOU DO? SAY IT! Min- at the doctors I made sure they told her she was pregnant, wanted to see the high hopes on your face. They injected her with a liquid that kills the baby, but she didn't know of course. Jake- AHHHH!!

I was beating him to death. I wasn't stopping at all, this was going to be the last time I saw him alive. Just how he wanted to see me suffer is how it's going to be for him.

My man came and I made sure he got it good. He will suffer too, now the only thing I could think about is how me and y/n were going to have a family together.

That's something I wanted with her one day. But it was taken away from us, even if the baby wasn't fully developed it still hurts so much.

I don't even want to tell her but I learned my lesson about not telling her things. She should know but when it's the right time. For now she should get better.

Before I handled business I asked how long it would take before she woke up. It was going to be soon so instead I sent my man to go handle this business.

I stayed by her side until she finally woke up which was later. She was getting out of the medication they gave her, her senses came back to her.

Y/n- what happened jake to our baby? Jake- I won't keep this from you but I think you should eat first okay? Y/n- Jake please just tell me.

Just keep arguing back to her wouodnt convince her so I got up and cupped her face. " I want you to be healthy, you look weak my love. I want the best for you so I'll feed you"

I went to get her something healthy to eat. And came back to see her with an unhappy face, when I walked in her eyes lit up. I fed her as she talked about how she would love to raise her first kid.

Deep down it shredded my heart into pieces, I really was having second thoughts of telling her. But at then end of the day I couldn't let her continue thinking she had a baby inside her.

I really didn't want her to freak out and loose her mind. She would go into a state that I couldn't bare to see, instead of distancing myself from her, I should've been there even if she was angry at me.

Later:

After she had eaten very well, she kept insisting I told her. That's the only thing she had in mind, I understood her.

Jake- the doctor was right y/n, no heartbeat... no baby. You were pregnant at some point but the baby died... it was killed. Y/n- what? By what? Or who? What caused this? Jake- min... he didn't want to see me happy with you by your side, he took our baby away from us. They injected a liquid to kill the baby.Y/n- that's why I was feeling sick, this whos time I thought it was pregnancy sickness.

She had nothing else to say. She laid back on the bed and closed her eyes. " will you still be by my side Jake?" She asked

My heart lit up because that's the only thing I wanted in life now. Jake- no matter what y/n I want to be with you forever, I promise you. Y/n- heal my heart please.

I'll be your healer □

Twenty six

I was grateful she took this better, I don't blame her for any other she would've. She was supposed to say the night at the hospital but she really did want to leave.

She didn't even know where she wanted to go. I felt at guilt because apart of her feeling sad was me. I was a cause of it, " I guess it wasn't the right time you know" she said

She was just walking and followed behind her. It said things there and then but I stayed quiet a few times. " I think I should take you home to your parents, they can actually be there and help you"

She stopped walking but didn't turn around" when I told you I wanted you to be by my side and heal me this is what I mean. " she said in a tone where she sounded like she was about to cry.

Y/n- they took our baby away from us jake! You think we should hide in the damn dark and fucking do nothing about it? Jake- y/n I know but your not in the right mind Y/n- take me to him! Jake- y.n no- Y/n- TAKE ME TO HIM!!!! TAKE ME .... Just take me gosh

And so I did

The whole car ride over there it's like she was talking to herself or coming up with a plan. Even I was afraid of her at the moment, for this exact reason I kept him alive.

I wanted to torture him but honestly I feel like y/n is going too. When we got there she got out the car and sped walk to the house.

I rushed right behind her as we went into the basement, where he was tied to a chair. Y/n saw a metal pipe and picked up, she was hesitant at first but everything came to her head.

She was able to recall everything he did to her. She swung hitting him, until she was tired. I pulled her away. If I let her continue she would really kill him and I don't want her to later ok regret it.

Y/n- WHYYY??? you had no damn right to kill my baby Min- (gasping) .... It was as big as a damn seed. Is that really what your beating me for? Y/n- should I answer your question by hitting you more? Because you got it right!

She was pacing around the room. Knowing she had him right in front her she didn't have the nerve to kill him or so I thought so. She took my gun from my hand but I stopped her, I back hugged her and whispered in her ear to stop.

Y/n- let me jakeJake- this is not you y/n, don't t turn out this way. I told you to never get your hands dirty especially not on this motherfucker. Let me knowY/n- I can't anymore.... Kill him then do it. Jake- I don't want you to be one the room. Y/n- fucking KILL HIM!

I looked at her because I worried for her. She wasn't even caring about my feelings, I knew how much this would affect her. I made my man take her out of the room and lock her in our bedroom.

I heard her yelling and fighting back but this is the only way it could be done. I pulled the trigger and put the gun to his forehead.

Jake- any last words? Min- you're parents are just as cruel as me, they knew about her pregnancy and agreed to kill it. Jake- what are you talking about they wouodnt take things that far? Min- are they even your real parents? Your walking on lies Jake, I know more than you think. Jake- you fucking bastard doing this to save yourself. Why can't you just tell me it all. Min- and why you understand it was supposed to be me and y/n. You came around and ruined things.

Y/n pov

I was waiting to hear multiple gunshots but time passed and not one did I hear. I needed to calm myself down, jake was right I'm not like this.

I called my brother to tell him everything. He wanted me to come hom but for some reason I wanted to be by Jake's side.

I had a feeling something bad happened or was going to happen. I went into the bathroom to look at myself, why was I this devastated.

I broke down in tears and fell on the bathroom floor. I was hurting so bad, my life was slowly falling into millions of pieces I thought had been finished into a puzzle when I met jake.

Someone entered the bedroom but I didn't care I cried and cried. Jake ran into the bathroom and hugged me, tightly and telling me things were going to be okay.

He wiped my tears off and planted many kisses on my face. Reassuring me enough for me to stop crying and stop and listen to him.

Jake- we need min alive ok but just listen to me. It's beneficial for us, I'm putting the pieces together and it all adds up. Y/n- what's happening now?

Jake- there's some business I have to handle, I don't want you to stay alone. I'll drop you off home yeah? Y/n- I want to go with you.Jake- I was afraid you were going to tell me that but this time it's really serious I need to go alone. With your parents I'll know your at least yea.

And so I agreed because at the end he shouldn't have to worry much right now. He quickly dropped me off home but before I got out the car he held my hand.

Jake- you're still me fiancé, stay safe and.. I love.. you

He pulled me in for a kiss and lasted longer than ever. And like again gave me a kiss on the forehead, and then left.

My brother stormed for me outside and got me inside quickly. He then shut and locked the door, " what's happening? " I asked

Brother- Fucking war

War?

Twenty seven

Y/n- war? What are you talking about? Brother- I'm gonna protect you until jake comes back. His parents declared war on him. Y/n- well this cant be happening! There should be another way!Brother- what other way? For you and him to die and give up like that? We defend no matter what! Y/n- where's mom and dad! Brother- they fled from here. I gave them a lot of the money I had saved up. We can't risk anything right now, you too need to learn how to shoot.

For a while my brother was teaching me how to shoot and gun properly. He was really impressed on my skills, and just taught me defense moves.

I was worrying for Jake where could he have gone now. " focus y/n! " my brother said but I couldn't. I wasn't at ease with this all happening.

Y/n- get out of here too. Leave with mom and dad, I can't risk to loose you so go. Brother- I'm fighting by your side y/n. I won't let you die, so protect me too. Y/n- thank you Julius. We will do our best.

Jake pov I was furious

More than I could imagine. Knowing my parents wanted to go against me was the least thing I expected. I was aware of my surroundings but we needed to have a quick talk.

I barged through the doors and straight into their meeting room. " SAY IT ALL TO ME NOW" I yelled at them. They were calm and ignored my presence, my father placed his cup of whiskey down and slowly walked over to me.

He stood in front of me and then slapped me. It was pretty rough it knocked me to the floor. I got back up and stared eight at him.

Father- you're no son to me, coming here to disrespect us like that. Preferring some civilian girl over us! Over being a Mafia. Jake- ALL I DID WAS TRY TO MAKE YOU PROUD! But there wasn't a thing I did that impressed you, I'm tired of it so let's fucking go. Mother- we would prefer min as a son! Jake- isn't he your son? The older brother you never told me about? Yea I went through the box full of letters that he would send you every week. I tried to feel bad for him.

The letters contained a lot of things that made me feel bad for him. But after every incident me and him had together slowly made me hate him even more.

I tried to forget about the letters but after coming across one where he said he was going to take me over. He wasn't lying at all, he really did come and ruin it all for me.

Father- Jake. Me and your mother will forgive you if you marry a girl. One of our closest friends is looking for an arranged marriage for their daughter. We would appreciate you if you could sacrifice yourself for this.

I legitimately almsot grabbed the bottle of whiskey to smash it on him. I was done sacrificing myself for them, my whole life they wanted it their way. Not anymore and nor would I ever marry any other girl if it's not y/n.

Jake- I'm not even feeling sorry at the moment nor do I have to think about it because my answer is no! Mother- Jake, you don't want this for yourself. You really want us to end your life? All of it will go to trash think about it. Jake- Go ahead. But I rather loose it all then loose y/n. I'm done with both of you controlling me.

There was nothing mroe to talk about with them. I got up to leave but my father spoke. " you walk out those doors without agreeing to the marriage and that girl dies"

Jake- I dare you to try. I'm not afraid of putting a damn bullet through your head.

And I left it at that

I slammed the doors shut and got into my car. I immediately went to y/n and her brother. She could really put her skills to use this time, her brother knew the minds of mafia so I knew she could be safe with him.

When I got there she hugged me right away. She examined me to see if I was hurt but I wasn't. " you need to stop doing this" she gave me a worried look

Jake- I promise I'll stop after I make sure your surely safe my love Julius- so what now? We go on a killing spree? Jake- they threatened me but I really need to know if it's for sure. I have my man they'll inform me.

Y/n had cooked us super delicious food, this was our moment to relax and enjoy. Afterwards she showed me her room, there was the purse I had sent her. She had kept it after all this time.

All the lights in the house were off for safety reason. The moon was shining through her window so I could still sort of see her.

She had sat on the edge of the bed and I wanted to feel her touch again, I wanted to feel even more loved by her. Feel her kisses again before I could loose it all.

I got in front of her and pushed her back on the bed, hovering over her. Kissing her hungrily, " my brother is in the house too" she said and it made me chuckle

Jake- guess we'll have to be quiet then Y/n- how if you go rough Jake- you got this princess SMUT WARNING!!!!!!!!!! (SHORT) We got more on the bed where i unbuttoned her shirt revealing her bare chest. I licked her breast and well as sucked them, she was trying so hard to stay quiet.

Planting kisses on her stomach when I reach her joggers , I wasted no time in taking them off. Along with her underwear. I grab her legs and pulled her closer to me spreading her legs open.

And inserting myself in her. She was so tight but pleasing for the both of us, I was thrusting back and forth so fast I had to control myself too.

I pulled her to the edge of the bed as I got my knees, I made sure she enjoyed this a lot.

We had more fun but we had to stop since I was getting a call from my gang members. We got cleaned up and changed, she tried getting up but her legs were shaking.

Twenty eight

Guard- your mother got other people involved to kill you. Jake- she's really taking it this far, I won't hold back then. Things are going to go this way then. Guard- what would you like us to do next. Jake- find out exactly plan.

There was nothing much else we could do but wait. All this occurring never in a million years did I think they would do this me. I should've known since I came across those letters, things weren't going to end well.

They wanted me to find a wife, loving and caring to me. But even then they weren't happy with the choice I made. They pretended and I fell into their trap just as y/n fell into mine.

I regret hurting a gorgeous girl like her. But this is the moment when I show her how much I love and care for her. Even if it means I have to loose my life for her.

We went through the many possible options that they could pull and how we would strike back. " if they want to bring other people into this then I can too, and she won't like who I bring in" I said to y/n and her brother

Julius- don't tell me you're getting who I think it is. Jake- he'll take my side anytime. Especially since he's been in the past with my parents not totally in good ways. Y/n- how would this even happen? I mean you guys cant just go on the street and start shooting at each other.Julius- The Mafia way!

I smirked at Julius because he was surely right. There were multiple ways to figure this out, all I was waiting for was my mothers or father call.

Maybe they would do this with poker, drugs, shooting range or just come storm the house. We had to be ready for anything.

Y/n- is this all because of me? Jake- even if it wasn't I'm fighting back Julius- your phone is ringing

It was my mother...

Mother- Jake son please, your father isn't in the room but I don't want us to fight. I love you equally to your brother. Jake- No you don't, because if you did you would not be afraid to say that in front of my father. Mom- Jake please I don't want you two killing each other. I'm hurting inside too. Jake- oh really because everything you wrote back to min didn't seem like you were hurting more glad I was old enough to leave your sight. Mom- it wasn't me who wrote those it was your father, he tortures me, he'll kill me if I go against him.

That did sound like my father, just form her voice I could tell she was hurting. But I was cautious and ware that this could be a setup. " how would I know you're not lying to me? I can't put myself at risk like that"

Mother- He's planning to storm y/n's house!

While my mother was telling me everything I got us out of there. I drove us to somewhere else. " he's main goal is to take away your biggest prize.... Her" my fist balled up in anger

Of course he would do that to me. To make me miserable again, to watch me fail right below his feet. Not even in my grave would he stop making me suffer.

Jake- I'm going for you momma, I'll get you out of that hell Mother- be careful son, whatever happens I love you.

I threw my phone out the window since it was a backup phone. He would definitely find out we had a call together and try to track the phone.

I looked at y/n through the mirror and she didn't seem like herself. She just wasn't use to this and I understood being in her position.

But not having her by my side bothered me. I would never forgive myself if something happened to her and I wasn't there to defend her.

I would storm his house. This was a battle between me and my father. He never showed love or affection so I guess we put an end to this.

I called up for backup of course in case of anything. Sorting out a plan on how we are going to attack. I'm not sure if he's expecting this but he sure should be ready to die.

He arrived and I told y/n to wait in the car and hide. I got into position and escorted in, I would assume my mother was upstairs hiding.

My goals were to save my mother and kill the guy who never had the title of a father. We had a shoot out with each other, my man and my father's man.

Jake- PULL IN!!! PULLL IN!!!

I shot the guards at the door, then shot the door open. But of course there would be more guards waiting inside. We threw smoke bombs inside and that made they shoot everywhere.

We took cover until they stopped shooting. This was for my snipers they would kill them. This would then clear our way to get inside but that's what they thought I would do.

Me and a few others went through the back and entered through there. Killing every man that got in the way. My father was standing on the stairs, luckily one of my guys pulled me out of the way.

He was shooting our way." IMMA KILL YOU JAKE!! AND THE BITCH" I didn't care much if he disrespected me because he was no one to me. But when he says something about y/n like that. Then it becomes a problem

FATHER- POP YOUR HEAD OUT LETS END IT NOWI shot his way which made him hide. I don't really think he thought through that he stood no chance against me. He did basically raise me but I became a man myself.

I got on the radio

Jake- The rest are upstairs, we have to push! Anderson- you really are one crazy motherfuckerJake- not as crazy as what you've done. Anderson- let's end this fucker forever!

Anderson seemed mroe excited then me to kill my father. Definitely because of the pasta events they had together, my father backstabbing Anderson.

Let's end it!

Twenty nine

We kept battling between each other when me and Andersons gang rushed upstairs. It was a pretty big house so it was pretty challenging.

I could see my mother from afar since was yelling and crying for my father to stop this all. But of course not a word from her could end this.

We just kept shooting at each other, knocking down man left and right. And when my father noticed all his man were down and he had run out of bullets.

He threw the gun at us and jump out the window. I ran to go and shoot him but he had fled before I could get to him.

Andersons made sure there weren't no more man. I went to my mother who was tearing up badly. She was so scared since any bullet could honestly have hit her.

Mother- I'm sorry Jake. I'm putting you through this. Jake- it's not your fault. My father for all these years made it his way. I know you were scared to say the truth, now I've come to save you. Mother- I'm lost for words my son. Jake- let's take back everything he took from us.

I knew he had a lot of valuable things here. We spent a good time looking for it all. Y/n even came and started helping us look for them.

I had a fear he would come back so I kept the house on lockdown. My mother was packing all of her stuff while I had my man gathering all of information we could use.

Y/n- you didn't get a chance to shoot him? Jake- he fled before I could, I won't be at peace if I don't kill him myself. Y/n- don't stress about it too much. Jake- I know and just being in here gives me nightmares. My whole childhood was in this house.Y/n- we'll make him remember who you truly are.

The police was near by and pretty sure coming over here so we left the house. My father house was now invaded by the police and swat team later accompanied by the FBI.

We were watching from afar, we went to one of my hide out places. Only close people know this spot but after getting information we needed. We were able to use it against him.

I still wonder where he could have gone. I need to find him and end his life. I was so eager that y/n tried calming me down.

Y/n- sit down, you're going insane Jake. Jake- that's because I am! All I wanted was him dead now he's somewhere roaming the streets.

I had ordered my men to go search for the money my father had stolen from me all these years and find that guy. I couldn't let him kill my mother or y/n, if it took to kill me to leave them at peace then it should be that way.

Y/n said she was going to go get us something to eat for us to clam down. I had a bad feeling of something, I didn't want to let her go but she insisted she would be fine.

My mother was looking at me and mins baby pictures, me and him looked so like. Just form seeing the pictures we looked so happy back then.

What went wrong?

When I had turned 18 my father had put me in the Mafia business. They gave me the title of the youngest mafia millionaire. We were wanted by many police but they never stood a chance against us.

I had always thought I was an only child but after all the time knowing min was my older brother just frustrates me. " I wanted to tell you that you had a brother but your father would've killed me if I did" my mom said

I want revenged for what he did to me and my mother. I felt like min was taking his side and they probably are thinking of something to attack me.

Mother- I never wanted bad to happen to you, but my opinion wasn't valid to your father. I wanted to run away and take you with me but he would find us and it would go bad for us two. Everytime I defended you he would beat me until I understood.

Jake- why was I born then? Mother- it was accidental, when he found out he went crazy since he only wanted one son to take the throne.

There were many questions I had but yet so many little answers. The was a big circle that never closed through out the years of why he didn't love me.

I went out to take a break because I felt like crying but I felt to embarrassed in front of my mother. Feeling weak felt like not an option, my father put that mindset in me.

I took many breaths and went back in to hug my mother. We hugged for a very long time and I never wanted to let go. She was warm and filled my heart up to feel better.

I heard things moving around but my mind was only in my mother. This is all I needed love from my mother after all. As soon as we were about to back up...

Al that echoed through the room

BAM!!

Thirty

The hug between me and my mother felt so long but yet so short. Her warmth truly made me feel loved and safe with her.

It all ended when a gunshot went off

BAM

My heart dropped so low just getting ready to feel the pain from the bullet going through. But after a few seconds I felt nothing, maybe one of my man shot their gun on accident

And I was just overthinking. When my mothers are aren't wrapped around me anymore. I felt as her figure slowly went downwards.

I caught her as blood was coming out of her mouth. We both ended up on the floor, she was bleeding out badly. I just thought to myself. NO NO no this can't be happening.

Jake- NO.... No... no no no

Who did this!? As I shifted me head to look up, my heart dropped once again.

My father....

He had a gun aimed at us as I pleaded for my mother to respond to me. She was unconscious but I didn't care. I pleaded and pleaded for her to wake up but after a bit no response.

Jake- WHYYYY!!! WHYY WOULD YOU DO THIS TO ME????? YOU KEEP FUCKING RUINING MY LIFE!!!!

I was yelling at the top. Letting my anger out, and he stood there in front of me with the biggest smirk. Him and his shadow over powered me. I felt defeated once again, I failed to protect my mom.

I felt so stupid and afraid

I was pressing down on my mother bullet womb to stop it from bleeding, but yet again I could only do so much to help her. As a second went by time was being wasted and I knew she could be gone anytime now.

Father- I never wanted you born. But yet again I was slightly happier you were a boy, someone to take the throne right. But you became useless, never did things my way. I hated that and so min just was the better son. Jake- I won't regret doing things my way. I eventually became more successful than you! I always thought why you never loved but now I don't need you or your love. But for you to come and take away one of the most precious people from me! You're gonna suffer and rot in hell.

Father- you'll be gone first

There was no way I could defend myself at this point so I just accepted the moment. I hugged my mothers lifeless body since it was already too late to try and save her. Closed my eyes and got ready.

Then waited to hear the gun to go off. But then nothing, I opened my eyes to see my father aiming the gun somewhere else.

I looked to the way and see y/n aiming a gun at my father. They were having this intense battle, I was covered with blood everywhere and I was hurting so bad right now.

Jake- STOP! DONT YOU DARE SHOOT HER TOO!! Father- She was my main target, the one all along to kill her. You could've been more without this bitch. Y/n- and you could've been a better dad, but yet then seeing one of your sons do better than you in business and get all the deals truly bothered you. Step up your game next time! Father- you just run your mouth, this is why you lost the baby HAHHA!

I saw the anger in y/ns eye, but especially loosing a mother was one of the worst pains anyone could experience. I was crying with blood all over my face.

My father then slowly aimed the gun at me which made y/n try and cover me. I thought he would shoot me but he tricked y/n and shot her twice.

My eyes widened at the view right in front of me. I gasped like I couldn't breath, I yelled no so many times. I kept going back in forth not knowing who to hold.

My mother or y/n

Jake- WHYYYYYYY!!!!!! AHHHHHH YOU FUCKER WHY WHY WHY

I was soaked in blood from both of them. I felt useless, everything he said about me felt so true. All the insults felt like knifes stabbing me all over my body.

I was waiting for my turn. For him to shoot me in the head like he wished too. " I've won again jake, maybe next time listen to the boss " my father said

He put the gun on my forehead, Rifht as I looked up at him. I didn't want him to be the last person I see before I die but I didn't want to look weak to him.

GUNSHOT

Thirty one

G UNSHOT*****

I thought I had a bullet through my head. But instead seeing my father fall to the ground as he was the one who had a bullet through his head. It was instant death for him.

I was shaking badly and looking over I see Min still holding up the gun. As he realizes I'm looking over him, I knew I looked dead and exhausted.

He put his gun away and many man came in to carry our mother and y/n out the room. He then came in front of and got on his knees. I didn't know what to expect from him at all, hate too?

A hug

He hugged me tight. And then wiped the blood off my face, " there's no time for me to apologize properly, mom and y/n need us" he grabbed my hand and pulled me.

Min- you know the power you hold stay strong for them Jake- I..... why are you helping us? They're gone and I might as well die too.

He stopped and grabbed me by my collar " say that shit again, they NEED YOU! " min said to me

He was right I needed to stop having these thoughts and gain strength. And so I did, we got into the car and drove straight and fast to the hospital they were in.

I didn't have high hopes at all for the both of them. But I still wanted to keep the little faith I had left in me. Min talked to me and honestly it did really help me.

Life wasn't worth it with them two not in it. Other things I thought were why did min kill our father and not me. Or how did he escape from the basement.

The nurses helped clean me up and check me, I was just weak and tired. So they gave me a IV to feel better, a therapist came into my room and talked to me.

I think min had told her everything and I would just fill her in with the rest. I didn't want to talk to anyone, didn't want to hear anybody's voice.

I wanted to hear y/ns and my mothers. I was just waiting for them to tell me that they were dead and they could do nothing anymore.

Therapists- a lot occurred tonight Jake. What is something heavy you want to get off your chest? Jake- he could've killed me instead of them! Therapist- how was your father like? Jake- Fucking monster, mentally and physically abused me and my mother. Therapists- did you try to run away? Or get help? Jake- He's a Mafia, what do you think? Bullet straight through your head.

I think that honestly startled the therapists because she said she would be back but she never came back. I got up from the bed and went to go check up on the others.

Min- you should've stayed in the bed!Jake- and become miserable?

Both y/n and my mother were in surgery and afterwards connected with all types of wires. I didn't even want to look at them knowing I couldn't save them.

Let them die in front of me. I'm a liar. I promised and broke the promise I made. " they are going to be proud no matter what. You'll feel their love all the time" he was telling me like they were going to die soon

I kept telling myself they're going live and everything. That's when the doctor came out to talk to us.

Doctor- besides the fact that you guys come here often, your mother lost an insanely amount of blood and in this case it becomes difficult for us to prevent death. But it looks like she's fighting better than I have ever seen. We gave her blood right away and well we will evaluate her. Uhh but for the lady, she was shot twice and even after surgery she's fighting for her life and ... might not make it.

I ripped the iv out of my arm and went insane. I got good and bad news but I wasn't taking it well at all. Everyone was telling to stop and clam down.

Doctor- Boss your lady can get through it. Just have faith! Jake- Save her.... SAVE HERR!!!! I CANT LOOSE HER A SECOND TIME.

The first time was her not wanting to talk to me. But now this was different she could actually be gone fork my side. This would be my biggest night- mare of all.

I'll keep faith

Thirty two

I t was a constant of waiting game. A few days went by and my mother had the energy to finally wake up. She was resting and building up her strength. But on the other hand y/n still hadn't woken up.

I sat by her side day and night telling her things but it felt like I was talking to myself. I hated myself everyday just seeing her on that bed fighting for her life.

I hung my head low but still held her hand. " if you really can't keep fighting, you can't rest in peace. " I said to her

I felt something pressing on my finger but I didn't bother to check what it was. Then like a tap on my hand, then it turned into multiple taps.

Her finger..... her hand was moving...!!!

I jumped out of the chair and ran to the doctor, yelling that she was awake and moving. They rushed in and examined her and it was like a miracle.

My heart was pumping so fast because of how excited I was. " for now we will examine her and run tests again" so then yet again I had to wait again.

So after a bit I was the first one to see her. I felt nervous going inside knowing that this time she was actually awake. I' didn't know if to hug her or kiss her or just admire my baby.

I peeked in and she noticed right away giving me a huge smile. She could barely move since well it would cause her a lot of pain. I stopped myself from hugging her and all.

I still questioned to myself And everyone how this was even possible. I was very thankful that she survived through this and knew she was stronger then me.

Y/n- how are you doing? Jake- I'm holding up just alright still coping through it all. Y/n- you did well jake. You were put in a tough situation of your mother and me. Also how is she? Jake- she made it too.Y/n- how'd you even manage too save us both or get us here? Jake- it wasn't me..... it was min

She gave me a confused look and it was understandable why she gave me that look. " he hasn't told me why he helped me, he was the one who killed our father. So basically he saved us three" I said to her

It was a conversation going back and forth of confusion. It was good to see her awake and recovering just fine. I don't want to ever loose them Ive felt too much pain.

My heart still aches, many stab whoms that still haven't healed.

I let her rest for a bit and went back out to get startled by min. He was leaning against the wall I guess waiting for me to come out.

Min- how is she doing? Jake- alright, recovering from two shots. Min- keep them safe this time. I won't be around anymore, it doesn't mean because I helped you, you won't have enemies. Jake- I gained more enemies? Who exactly? Min- don't stress about it right now. Here's my number if you need anything but I can't promise I'll come to your rescue.

Take care of both of them for me yea?

He then left. I sat on the floor running my fingers through my hair because it definitely was dometjing to stress about. I would have to set the hospital on high alert of protection.

I'm not weak anymore. My biggest worry was my father but I let fear and anyone get to me. That's over with forever, I'm the new Mafia king.

I had my head hung low and all I saw was a women's heels clicking against the floor coming right at me. " you really are miserable" I haven't heard this voice in a very long time.

But I still couldn't recognize whos it was. I looked up and even then I didn't know. " how come you turned down my request for an arranged marriage for the both of us? We would've been such a powerful couple" she stated

The girl they tried setting me up with.

Jake- Whyd you come? To beg me? Women- I'd only beg you yea. Why are you even here? Jake- No is the answer so you can leave now.

She smirked at me and pulled me to get up. " you aren't that bad, I'm surprised your single"

Jake- I'm not Women- I see now, it all makes sense. Rumors sure do spread fast and become true

She got closer to me and JSUT smelled me." I'll give you an actual kid who makes it " i instantly grabbed her by the neck and squeezed it as hard as I could.

People pulled me back and off her but that really set me off. " call me...(cough) I'm always available " i charged at her but I was dragged back.

Thirty three

Y /n pov

I was laying in the hospital bed very exhausted and in pain. I needed to pee so went to the bathroom but very slowly dometjing caught my attention from outside.

There was a window in my room so I went closer. It was jake and another girl, they were very close to each other and that's all I wanted to see.

I went to the bathroom and got changed into my clothes, I knew I shouldn't be going anywhere but I felt hurt. After saving me each time he probably got tired of me.

The hospital room was connected to the hallway so I went through. I laid my head low and tried to seem as normal as I could.

Thank goodness no one noticied me. I had my phone so I called my my brother, my parents were still in another country right now.

Julius came for me and knew about what had happened. He helped me to the car and I told him to drive off, I hadn't told him why I was leaving and without Jake.

I don't think I'm fit for this mafia world.

Brother- what's happening now? Y/n- let's leave. Go to mom and dad and be at peaceBrother- we need to get tickets then, but are you sure? Without Jake Y/n- yes without him and everyone else. I want it to be like it was before. Brother- y/n jake loves you to death! Why are you trying to run away from him? Y/n- he was with another girl. Im fucking done Brother- what if it's not like that, you probably only saw for like three seconds. We're going back!

He turned the car around and called jake. They were all looking for me. I kept yelling at my brother to not but he was the one behind the wheel so it was pointless.

When we pulled back into the parking lot I could see jake running around looking everyone. I know he was looking for me, but I felt stupid maybe my brother was right I was just over exaggerating.

Brother- let's come up with a clean story Y/n- mom and dad came back but after about left again Brother- he would believe that? Y/n- the way we say it then yes

There we got out of the car Julius helping me and Jake spotted us right away. He came running as he tried catching his breath at the same time.

Jake- where'd you go? You disappeared and I was worried looking every-where for you! Y/n- I'm sorry, my parents came back but left again so I wanted to see them you know Jake- you didn't even let me know. I thought of too many things and not good ones Y/n- I'm sorry

I didn't want to be in the hospital anymore and I knew I was putting myself at risk but it was for the better. We went to Jake's safe house which was huge would expect it.

I rested in bed a few days until I got my energy and strength back. These days have been hard jake had rarely talked to me and I wasn't sure why. I always jumped to conclusions so I let it be

And the few times a day I got to see him he just looked stressed and worried. I tried asking him but he avoided that topic with me.

Y/n- jake! Dometjing is wrong so what is it? Why do you keep avoiding me huh? Jake- that's not what I'm trying to do. I don't know what you mean? Y/n- you think I'm stupid? I see it all you see me like five minutes per day!!! Jake- I'm busy y/n..Y/n- so for what reason did you want me back if you knew you would be busy? I'm just in your damn way I shall Then excuse myself

I grabbed my phone anf bag and tried leaving the door but he grabbed my wrist pulling back very hard. " Where are you going now? "

Y/n- away from you! I'm making your pathway clear Jake- Can you stop being so dramatic, I have long days and come back to this? Y/n- So are you just not gonna try and think of how I felt? I've been in this fucking room ALONE for I don't know how many fucking days!!!! Jake- so it's now my fault? You were resting what did you want to do? Y/n- That's the stupidest shit you could honestly tell me! I should've left when I had that chance, you know in fact who was that girl in the hospital? Y'all were all up on each other!

He chuckled but very sarcastically like making fun of me. " you saw? "   I said " not on purpose but thank goodness I did, you did already so much. Protecting me my ass"

Jake- You want to go there? Y/n- I JUST DID! You don't want to tell me what the hell is wrong I'm trying to support you but you push me away so I'll end it by going far away

Jake- Fine! Then leave i just worried too much about caring for someone like you. You couldn't even keep our child safe !

I stopped anything i was doing my heart dropped and tears came out of my face almost immetiaoy. We were hurting each other with words but I think he took it too far.

Y/n- you weren't even the dad anyways..

I sped to the door and left crying. Running down the stairs and out the house, I was in some rich neighborhood so I didn't know where I was. I kept calling my brother but he was picking up.

I called my mother and she answered. " I'm going home. To you guys"

Thirty- four

I just walked down the side walk since I had no ride. I was out of my mind and didn't know what to do or where to go. That's when I hear someone calling my name and form the voice it was jake

He kept yelling for me to stop but I didn't. I just kept walking and walking until he ran up to me.

Jake- what do you mean I wasn't the father? Y/n- is that really what you came to bother me with? Are you not aware of what you literally told me just before that!? Jake- I'm such an idiot and I didn't mean it at all, Can you please just listen to me. Can we talk this out? Y/n- so you can insult me and treat me like shit? All I wanted was to support you! All I did was ask what was wrong! Jake- I'm getting married to someone else y/n.

I stopped my thoughts and I really thought there was nothing more I could hear that could break my heart more than it already was. I started hitting him as I cried and let it all out.

He had let me hit it but then he grabbed my wrists for me to stop, I fell to the ground in disbelief. How could he just tell me do calmly like it wasn't a big deal.

Y/n- why?.... WHYYYY?? Jake- I have too. Y/n- Okay go live your life happily with another girl anf leave me alone!

Julius had finally came around the corner to pick me up he saw my condition and got worried. On the drive to the airport I explained everything to him.

Not leaving one bit out.

After all I guess I was just wasting my time. " move on, tjings like this happen in the mafia life. Wether you like it or not he's going to eventually have a family with that girl too. She probably holds a lot of power and is using it against him."

My brother said to me but I stayed WUIET I just stared out the window hurt. What did I do wrong?

I would expect him to fight bsck or refuse but I guess not this time. Maybe it was a sign for me to just let him be, I supported him way too long.

When we got to the airport my brother and I gave each other goodbyes. He couldn't come since he had tjings to still do here.

I got in the plane but before through everything he had given me away. I still had kept onto his ring but I would plan on selling it.

I would need money so.

It was a few hours in the air so I took a nap and rest without having to worry. Finally landing my parents were waiting for me. I went to thrm and felt safe in their hug.

Mother- you're finally home honey! Father- you can start a new life here okay.

Days later:

Being able to forget everything was not easy. My parents got me a therapist, it was helpful but I never expressed myself too much.

I got myself a job and really enjoyed. The people who worked here were so lovely too. Became friends and got close super fast. I told them my past situation and they were in shock.

They gave me good advice though. I wanted too focus on myself and become a better person. I never wish nothing bad on him but he can grow as a person himself and learn from his mistakes.

Loosing someone Loyal. I wanted to make him hurt when he told me SBOUT not keeping our baby safe and he is the dad but now he'll continue his life thinking he wasn't.

I was walking down an alley that had a river next to it and the cute ducks just swam around. In this town there were a bunch of people which was nice.

Everyone got along with each other. I heard yelling but it was normal until someone ran into me and we fell into the water.

I didn't know how to swim so I panicked and I guess the person realized and helped me stay on top of the water. It was a guy, grey eyes and cute smile.

He took me and helped me get up back on the road. We were both soaked in water and he apologized.

Guy- I'm sorry, I wasn't paying attention. I hope you won't get mad at me. Y/n- don't worry I'm fine. It's okay

We then parted ways I took a Quick Look again since I assumed he wouldn't but he did. We made eye contact he smiled and he had such cute dimples.

Reminded me of jake...

Jake pov This was the worst time of my life. I ruined it all snd I thought I had figured it out. Now she's gone so there's point in doing anything.

She had threatened me and got my grandparents involved. Everyone was against me so this was a way for me to be safe. And to keep y/n

It was a few days later since she was gone and today was the day I was getting married. I was getting ready but I wanted it to end already

Being at the end of the isle killed me. The one that should be walking down was y/n instead some other girl.

The same girl my dad wanted me to marry. And the one who came to the hospital. When she got to the end she whispered. " I get what I want. Next time listen "

We eventually got married. Husband and wife, when I looked up I saw my brother standing outside of the church with a disappointed look on his face.

He helped me for what!

When I got out he pulled me aside to talk to me. " you let slip out of your hands like that. I should've known you were useless and a piece of shit. She left a message for you. You can learn from your mistakes but not expect someone else to fix them for you, forget about her ever existing and move on. She wants nothing to do with you anf has a happy life now"

Jake- she found someone new? Brother- probably but I didn't ask. Be happy for her and honestly she's right. I'm not gonna be here no more for you manage your own tjings

Then he gave me a little chip. I went to my car and listen to it.

It was y/n...

Y/n- I don't know when youll hear this. But hopefully soon, you made me happy many times and I thank you for that. But I didn't deserve this at all, I should've known better then to be with you. Have a happy marriage and continue your life, your brother already left my message but once again never look for me. I'm better anf happier without you here, I will make a better life where I am. Hopefully she can give you a baby. - y/n

I screamed and yelled hitting the steering wheel. People looked at me like I was crazy.

And I was now.

No more her by my side, i can't let her go

Not that easy. She's mine...

She'll see me soon

THE END

The end of the book, My stalker is a Mafia. For everyone who got this far thank you for reading this stroy. Im pretty sure many of you will want a second psrt anf I will think about that. I hope you guys like this story! I will be coming out with a new book so make sure to check it out

The new book will be called

My Cold CEO Husband 21+

www.ingramcontent.com/pod-product-compliance
Lightning Source LLC
Chambersburg PA
CBHW070404200726
48294CB00003B/1076